The Lost Message

Gil Herman

Managing Horizons Press

Cover design by Jason Brashares.

Contents

Chapter 1

Destiny

Corrine Randall sits on a park bench in active pursuit of her destiny.

Despite the 70-degree weather, her dark gray overcoat smothers her body, making her seem frailer than her 120 pounds might appear. The pockets of the coat are stuffed with loose papers she's picked up from various places, some neatly folded, others wadded tightly as if to protect them against scrutiny or to keep their contents from eking out into the world. One pocket holds a cracked mobile phone, its battery completely drained after laying against a curb for several days, having been dropped by a teenaged girl who'd just broken up with her boyfriend. The tear beneath the left-hand pocket serves handily as another storage place, this one designated to hold the Swiss Army Knife, its large blade retaining only half of its former self. Corrine keeps the blade extended, believing that if she were attacked again, she'd be able to pull the knife quickly to defend herself.

The right sleeve of the coat also sported a long gash. Into this she stuffed her one black glove with holes in three fingers and a striped glove, clearly a size too big for her small hand, despite the missing thumb part. As often happens in the early Spring in Chicago, this was a day ranging about 10 degrees above normal. She knew she'd probably need the warmth the hand coverings offered that night when the sun was down as she desperately tried to catch moments of sleep on the hard benches along the path. Despite their missing parts, she knew it was unlikely to find a better set in the next few weeks until the weather turned and people started discarding the past winter's outerwear into their trash cans with intentions of purchasing a brand new and more stylish pair for next year. "That was the problem with fashion trends," she joked to herself. "I'm always a season behind waiting for the castaways of last season to find their way to *my* shopping mall."

Another fashion statement included an old pair of Reeboks. She'd been fortunate to find a matching pair that was only a half-size too large. The toilet tissues she'd stuffed in the toes and the newspaper covering the hole in the right sole made them a prized possession. She was quite satisfied with the comfort, both when pushing her cart along the paths of Millennium Park and with the warmth they provided, even on the coldest nights, their larger size affording her space to stuff more torn newsprint all around the sides and tops of her feet. This was particularly valuable because Corrine did not trust socks. She'd never even tried to wear one sock of the many she could have picked from, even from the classier neighborhoods. There was something about wearing someone else's socks – or underwear – that she felt was too personal. It was not because she was concerned with germs – she could always wash them out pretty thoroughly with help from a soap dispenser and sink at a public washroom. It was a fear that wearing the intimates of someone else would cause part of their essence to invade her own – and this was something she was desperately trying to maintain along with her sanity since she'd chosen to make the afternoon escape from her old apartment back east.

She wears what was once a bright red scarf wrapped loosely around the turned-up collar of the coat. She loves this scarf, having retrieved it three weeks ago from a wire trash bin lining the path along Michigan Avenue. Ignoring the eyes of fitness advocates jogging along the sidewalk, she had grabbed the scarf as one of the first accessories to her new life shortly after arriving in Chicago. Back then, she thought of it as her first disguise. Now it is a dear friend that helped her out in several tight situations. A large dried blood stain blending in with the color if not the texture, served as a reminder of an unfortunate encounter with a gang banger who sought to rob her of all her earthly possessions transported in the old roller cart with the wobbly back wheel.

She'd found the cart only two weeks after getting to Chicago. Certainly not a person to steal – not with her values – she was fortunate to find the cart in the alley behind the building at 8 South Michigan Avenue. Someone had likely used it to move materials around their office and abandoned it due to the broken back wheel. Corrine considered trying to find who owned it so she could return it. But then she worried they would accuse her of taking it – or worse – make her the subject of some heroic and ethical act published in the paper or mentioned as a news filler. She was certainly not going to risk that kind of exposure. *They* might see the story and track her down. Then her young life would be brought to an abrupt end.

Besides, the cart was clearly damaged, although not beyond repair. Someone would probably just throw it out in the garbage again anyway, so why not take it now without waiting for it to make itself available to her later? Over time, she'd found pieces of insulated electrical wires – cutoffs thrown from a construction site – and been able to thread them through the axle to reattach the wheel restoring it to a wobbly existence. At least she didn't have to pull the cart along always lifting the back right side at every crack in the sidewalk, not to mention the heavy lifting over every curb.

At first, all she had to transport in the cart was the small blue and yellow duffel bag into which she'd packed one change of clothes in her hasty departure. She'd lasted a scant week by changing back and forth between the clothes on her back and what she'd carried. Never having slept outdoors in her life – even a Girl Scout camping trip - she'd been ill-prepared for the devastation that occurs to one's clothes from constant wear 24 hours a day, especially the abrasion from wood and metal park benches.

She'd arrived in early Spring with unseasonably warm weather, so she had spent her first night simply sleeping on the grass in Millennium Park near the Jay Pritzker band shell. She hadn't understood how the temperature changed through the night and into early morning creating a dampness that soaked through to the marrow of her bones. She awoke that first morning more exhausted and chilled than when she'd suffered through a bad bout of the flu two years earlier. But at least she was alive and felt safer than she had in days.

Over those first couple weeks, she'd become acutely aware of homeless people – how they dressed, where they slept, what they ate – how they survived. She kept her distance and at the same time tried to soak up whatever she could learn through observation to help her acclimate to this new life she'd chosen. She started scouring trash bins and alleyways for anything that would help her make it through the day – and especially the night. She'd quickly overcome lifelong discomfort with being dirty and fears of rats, because a completely different lifestyle she believed was her best means to survival – however long it might take.

Corrine had established a routine to help her make it through the days. She believed living as a bag lady far from her place back east would be a sufficient disguise should anyone be looking for her. Homeless people were mostly invisible as long as they didn't try to interact with the normal people - the commuters, the walkers and joggers, and the people-watchers who hung out in the park during their work breaks. She kept to herself and her park benches. Her only interactions were with the pigeons that congregated around her, watching her and pecking at the ground for whatever tidbits might exist. Many times, she was able to find day-old bread behind a bakery on Michigan Avenue. She'd wrap it in discarded newspaper and put it in her cart on her way to today's bench. Once settled, she'd break the bread and scatter a few crumbs to whichever pigeons were in that area.

Over many weeks, she started to notice that there were a few pigeons that always seemed to find her wherever she settled for that day. She began to recognize some of them from the unique color patterns of their feathers. And then she gave them names.

The one who seemed to be in charge – pecking at others to keep them further away from the crumbs – had a solid grey pattern over most of its body except for what Corrine thought of as white epaulets at each shoulder where the wing met the body. She came to think of his behavior and attitude as being like the military, so she named him Commander.

A multi-colored pigeon just seemed to prance around, often looking to Commander for approval or protection. Corrine couldn't determine pigeon gender, but she thought this pigeon to be female and possibly romantically connected to Commander. She named her Princess.

A third that often showed up wherever Corrine settled, was mostly copper colored. She thought of that pigeon as Goldie.

The fully-white pigeon reminded her of a peace dove, so she named it Peace. Often as Commander cleared out a space around Corrine's bench with Princess following closely behind, Goldie and Peace seemed to stand guard to ensure no other pigeons approached Corrine without their approval.

After giving them names, it was a natural next step to talk to them while she tossed breadcrumbs in their direction. Since she could see they were protective of their territory in front of her, she would sometimes toss some crumbs to the side or behind the bench to be fair to the other pigeons that had gathered but were kept at bay by Commander's troops. When she did that, Commander would sometimes look at her and then at the other pigeons. He'd give his head a brief nod and go back to guarding his territory without running off the other birds. Corrine thought this very noble of him.

For the most part, people left Corrine alone. She was thought to be somewhat crazy just sitting on various benches, her broken pushcart to the side of the bench, feeding breadcrumbs to the pigeons and talking to them. Best to just leave her alone.

And she sat at her bench all day no matter the weather. She'd rescued an old poncho from a park trash bin and put it over her if it rained. She'd also found a full trash bag someone left near a receptacle. She emptied the trash into the receptacle, wondering what the problem with someone was that they couldn't throw away their trash, but grateful that she now had a good plastic bag. She turned it inside out and used it to cover her cherished possessions in the cart if ever needed. It served double duty sometimes as the bottom layer for a sleeping space on a damp bench or wet grass covered with newspaper or cardboard. She had also salvaged an old bicycle cord with no lock. At night, she would wrap that around her leg and then around the bottom of her cart. If someone tried to steal her cart, the movement would wake her very quickly.

Some days well-meaning, or just curious people would come by where Corrine had settled for the day. Almost everyone tried to have some kind of conversation with her, asking her name, if she felt safe, what her story was. She ignored them all and just mumbled and talked with the pigeons. Some people brought her things at times – a bottle of water, a sandwich, even a sleeping bag. Although she was grateful, she never displayed any signs of gratitude or even recognition. Most people just shook their heads and walked away believing her to be a beyond-hope crazy person.

She liked it that way.

Chapter 2

Young Trauma

Joshua Carpenter left the funeral service for his mother just a couple of hours ago. He was filled with complex love-hate emotions fed by years of living with her since early childhood to his now 25 years of life.

Josh never really knew Joe Carpenter, the man his mom married so he'd have a father figure in his life. He was away from home a lot serving in the Illinois National Guard around the state. In 2003, shortly after Josh's 5th birthday, Joe shipped out to Iraq as part of the 160,000 land troops that were part of the shock-and-awe engagement. He was a casualty of war leaving Josh's mom, Mary, a single parent. She was bitter about the deployment and loss of emotional and financial support. Mary and Josh downsized to an apartment in the east side of Oak Park.

Mary didn't make friends easily and she was overly protective of Josh. He had to come right home after school – no sports, or music, or other extracurricular activities. He wasn't allowed to have classmates over or to go to their homes either. He was kept fairly isolated.

Josh had a strong interest in computers and taught himself to do some programming. He became very good at it and was fascinated by his ability to learn several programming languages. His mom did let him use the internet to keep up to date with the news or watch streaming videos. He was not allowed to use social media or even email to connect with other people directly. All he could do was read about them in the third person. Through middle school, high school, and even college, he was pretty much a loner.

One life-impacting event took place shortly after his dad had shipped out. It turns out that Mary had a rare condition – anosmia – having a total lack of ability to smell. On this particular day, she was baking a meat loaf in the oven and left the room to attend to some other chores while listening to music through her headphones. Some sauce and cheese from last night's pizza had dripped on the oven racks and started a small smokey fire. Josh smelled the smoke but couldn't get his mom's attention. Just then, the neighbor from the next apartment knocked on the door saying she smelled smoke. Josh let her in, and she turned off the oven which allowed the fire to go out. Then she went to look for Josh's mom.

In the meantime, another neighbor must have smelled the smoke and had called 911. Fire engines and an ambulance, their sirens screaming, pulled up to his apartment building and pulled hoses out to connect to hydrants. Several firefighters ran in and pounded on the door. Mary, her ears still plugged, didn't hear the sirens and was unaware of the problem.

As the helpful neighbor approached Josh's mom to tell her about the situation, the neighbor heard the pounding on the door and got Josh's mom's attention just as the door was broken in. The firefighters checked to be sure everything was secure, but several raised their eyebrows in concern that the situation had even occurred. They questioned Josh's mom and the neighbor about the situation and whether something like this had ever happened before. Mary and the neighbor answered that this was the only time something like this had happened. As the neighbor was leaving, the firefighters thanked her for her alertness and ability to put the fire out.

Mary explained her anosmia problem and was reprimanded by the fire captain that it was therefore even more important to stay alert when she was cooking something, and especially not to leave the kitchen. She had put her child's life and her own and all her neighbors in danger. Mary thanked the firefighters and said she'd be more vigilant in the future.

A few days later, just as she was getting over the embarrassment of what had happened – and paying to get the door repaired – Mary answered another knock on the door. This time it was a social worker from the Department of Children and Family Services who, in a condescending and paternal voice, scolded Mary for allowing Josh to be put in danger. She was accused of being a neglectful mother and that the DCFS had opened a file to record any future abuse or neglect.

The additional embarrassment was overwhelming. She and Josh stayed in their apartment and isolated themselves from everyone. Eventually, a couple weeks later on a sunny afternoon, Mary took Josh for a walk through Austin Gardens. Josh leaned into a grouping of lilacs and bent a long branch toward his mom's nose and said, "Smell the pretty flower Mommy." Mary was furious and felt Josh was making fun of her inability to detect odors. So, she smacked him hard across his innocent face and forcibly dragged him out of the garden along the gravel path and bumped against large landscaping boulders.

He did not understand his mom's inability to smell and was confused and traumatized by her strong reaction.

From that day forward, Josh avoided being in parks or any open green spaces and especially stayed away from flowers.

So today, after the service for his mom, Josh decided for the first time in 20 years, that he was going to take a walk in the large park across from his workplace.

Chapter 3

Flash, Flesh and Fantasy

As on most days, as Corrine sits on a park bench mumbling and talking to the pigeons, she is also thinking about what brought her to this situation.

She was from the Mission Hill neighborhood in Boston. Mission Hill is a 3⁄4 square mile, poor residential neighborhood, bordered by Roxbury, Jamaica Plain and Fenway-Kenmore and the town of Brookline. Corrine's mom rented a two-room apartment off Tremont Street where she raised Corrine. Her mom held two jobs – one as a stocker and bagger at a grocery store from 6 am to 2 pm, the other as a waitress at a local diner from 3 pm to 11 pm. Corrine had to get herself to school and back each day, but spent many afternoons, dinner, and bedtime at the diner.

She was a quick learner in school and showed particular promise in science. She especially liked biology and thought about going into the medical field. Although she had good grades in high school and showed a lot of potential, money was too tight to consider a 4-year college. So, she enrolled at the Roxbury Community College (RCC), easily accessible by the MBTA Orange Line. She took a number of classes aiming for an Associate Degree as a Certified Nursing Assistant. And every day she rode the train she noticed other students heading to one of the Harvard Medical School campuses and fantasized about becoming a doctor someday.

One evening after classes she was sitting at the diner doing homework for her Introduction to Nursing and Healthcare class, she became aware of a shadow over her shoulder. She turned to meet the handsome face of a young policeman. He'd been a regular customer for months at the diner and she'd often caught him looking at her from a few tables away. Her mom had kidded her about him suggesting that he might be interested in talking with her but seemed a little hesitant. She was only just 19 and he was at least in his mid-twenties.

His curiosity had finally gotten the best of him, so he came over to see what she was working on. He introduced himself as Jude McBride and that he is a beat officer with the Boston Police Department, District B–3. He smiled and said, "I'm here to keep you safe."

She returned his smile and introduced herself. "I'm Corrine Randall and I'm a student at RCC studying nursing and healthcare. Someday I'll keep people safe, too."

He seemed very interested that she was attending RCC and going into healthcare. Over the course of their conversation, she shared that she was also looking for parttime work, preferably where there was the opportunity to do some studying while on the job.

"I have a connection with a local store that needs a front desk receptionist," Jude told her. "I'd be happy to introduce you."

"Wow. That'd be great. Thank you, Jude," she exclaimed.

It turned out his connection was with an Adult Superstore not far from where they were sitting. The store, aptly named Flash, Flesh, and Fantasy, catered to adults looking for merchandise that might enhance their intimate encounters. The store offered items of interest to men, women and whatever leanings in the way of physical items with batteries, oils, lotions, self-administered "toys", and, of course, non- G-rated magazines and movies.

Now Corrine was no prude, but even she blushed a bit as she was given a tour of the merchandise and advised as to her responsibilities at the front desk. The owner told her, "You won't be expected to handle or discuss any of the merchandise but only direct patrons to the sections of the store they express interest in. You'll also answer the phone and respond to questions about store hours (24/7) or whether such-and-such an item was in stock." He added, "You won't even have to pay attention to security as we've hired a number of cops like Jude to mostly just be visible to discourage any undesired behaviors. "And," she thought, "the best part, when there are no customers, I can work on my studies and be paid well while minding the store."

She scheduled her flexible work hours to allow her to continue her education. Over the next several months, she and Jude started seeing each other outside of work and became a bit of an item. Even though the term sounded outdated, she thought of him as her boyfriend.

Over those first few months at the store she realized that they didn't just have movies for people to view in store or purchase. They also had a back entrance through which "stars" and clients could enter into a studio where they made pornographic movies. She figured, "It's really a separate business and they are only working with consenting adults. It's nothing I need to be involved with. And besides that, Jude and his cop friends are aware of it, so if there was anything illegal, they'd take care of it."

Corrine continued reviewing her memories. After about 6 months on the job, she was sitting at her station at the reception desk. There were no customers at the time, so she was quietly studying her schoolwork. She had turned off the ambient music so she could better concentrate without the sound. Sitting in the silence she heard some talking coming from the back area of the store where there was a door to the studio. The door must have been left open because she could make out the loud argument. The store owner was talking with Jude about some recent filming they'd done using young kids. Evidently the kids were street kids – runaways or throw-outs – that the police had picked up. Some of the kids were cleaned up and made to provide services to clients while being filmed. The argument was about the distribution of pay to the cops for procuring the kids and not talking about it. Jude was clearly the ringleader of the corrupt officers.

Just then, a customer came into the store. Jude and the store owner heard the buzzer indicating that the front door of the store had opened and then noticed they'd left the studio door partially open. They wondered if Corrine might have heard them talking.

"Don't worry," Jude said. "She might not have heard anything. If she did, I'll talk her down and tell her to keep quiet. If she won't, then I'll take care of it."

Corrine was flabbergasted! She had no idea they were producing child pornography and that her boyfriend was the leader of this corrupt enterprise. And now, she could sense the real threat that her new knowledge presented. She knew that she had to get out of there in a hurry. She didn't even bother to pack up her schoolwork but just ran out the door to get away.

She got near her apartment and noticed Jude's cruiser was parked out front. She panicked. She knew she had to disappear and leave everything behind. She had a little money on her and a bank card. She quickly went to the nearby Goodwill store and bought a pair of jeans, an extra-large sweatshirt and some undergarments, a pair of sneakers and socks along with a blue and yellow duffle bag in which to carry it all. She paid $34 of the cash she had so there would be no tracing of her bank card. Then she went to an ATM and used her bank card to withdraw all her savings, $403.27. She figured they could probably trace that use, but it was the final time she was going to use that card. She took her money and duffle bag with extra clothing and ran to the bus stop. She didn't dare use her transit card because that, too, might be traced. She got on the first bus to come by taking it from Forest Hills to Dedham. Eventually, she made her way to an entrance ramp to I95 with a sign scribbled on cardboard – "To New York or Bust". She appeared clean and was a pretty girl traveling alone, so it wasn't too long before she hitched a ride.

Her first ride dropped her in New London, Connecticut. The second in New Jersey near the expressway to connect to the PA turnpike. Some University of Miami students were returning after a break and took her all the way to Toledo. From Toledo she got a ride with a couple of nursing students in a Volkswagen hatchback with a large dog sharing the back seat. They were moving to Chicago to start their new jobs at Northwestern Hospital.

By then, tired of traveling, Corrine decided to make Chicago her new home. She found a park bench in Millennium Park and just lay down and slept for 12 hours.

After all the anonymous travel connections, she was still worried that Jude and his buddies might find her if she tried to establish herself with an apartment and a job. School was definitely out of the picture. She was running for her life. As she looked around the park at the many kinds of people, she decided that becoming a homeless bag lady would be a perfect disguise.

Chapter 4

The Park

As Josh exited the Aon Center and walked out to Randolph Street, his stomach clenched and his breathing was labored. He was experiencing mild agoraphobia heightened by the memories of his mother's slap from that time in Austin Gardens. He'd avoided outdoor spaces, especially parks, for years and now was about to enter a big one.

He thought about how after high school, he'd chosen to attend college at the University of Illinois, Chicago. He could take a bus from his home down Austin Boulevard, get on the Blue Line and exit at Halsted. Then it was a short walk through campus with only small plots of land between buildings, so it was mostly tolerable. Over four years he earned a bachelor's degree in Computer Science with minors in Psychology and Philosophy. He was particularly fascinated by the emergence of artificial intelligence to help make sense of almost infinite data and variables. This, coupled with his interest in psychology and philosophy, especially ethics, gave him a strong liberal arts foundation and a sense of direction for a career in big data analysis. He chose to stay on and earned a Master's degree in Computer Science with an emphasis on machine learning. After his post-graduate degree, he quickly accepted a job with a small company partnering with Microsoft working out of their offices in the Aon Center. Although many of their upper-floor workspaces and conference rooms looked out over Millennium Park, he requested an inside cubicle and would avoid looking out any windows where he would see the park.

Still fairly much a loner, he had developed a friendship with a co-worker, John Baptiste. Together, they worked on several AI- related projects having to do with climate change, gun control, and astronomy. They usually ate lunch together in the company's lunchroom. John often suggested during nice weather days that they take their lunch and eat outside in the park. Josh always declined, sharing enough of his history to have John no longer make that that suggestion.

So, the day of his mom's funeral, feeling liberated from his past, he decided to celebrate with a walk in the park. Josh crossed Randolph Street and walked down the path next to the Harris Dance Theater. He walked through the Jay Pritzker Pavilion and was relieved that there was just a large lawn, but not many flower areas. "One step at a time," he thought.

It was 2 o'clock in the afternoon so most of the business lunch breaks were over and people had returned to their offices. Having fewer people in the park made it slightly less unbearable for Josh to set out on his journey. Recalling that he'd been a loner – an introvert really – most of his life, not by a natural psychological makeup, but forced through his emotional upbringing, he decided he would try to engage with people as he wandered.

His first encounter was with a young man dressed in casual business attire who was walking back from his late lunch break. The man was obviously in a hurry and looking down as he was about to pass Josh.

"Good afternoon. I'm Josh and this is my first time in the park," said Josh as the man approached.

"Good for you!" the man snidely replied. "Have a nice day."

"Well, that didn't go so well," thought Josh. "But that man was clearly in a hurry. I'll try again."

The next person Josh encountered was another young man. Clearly, he was not heading back to work as he was more-or-less just turning in circles and singing an unrecognizable tune. He was dressed in torn jeans, wearing jogging shoes riddled with holes and no socks. He wore a T-shirt from The Grateful Dead that was covered with food stains and who knows what else. He had a head of unruly hair and an unevenly trimmed beard. His eyes appeared to be looking at something unseen and far away.

"Hi. I'm Josh and this is my first time in the park," he tried again.

"Cool dude!" came the reply. "The Park is my universe and I'm here with all my creatures," he said as he sort of twirled around and waved his arms as if to cover everything. "Would you like to buy some stuff?"

Josh had no idea what stuff the guy was trying to sell but had no desire to learn more. "No thanks. Have a nice day."

"You too, man. I'm here every day if you change your mind."

Josh walked on. Next, he happened upon a woman dressed in many layers of colorful clothing. She wore three hats piled high on her head barely covering numerous strands of unruly grey hair. She wore a golden sash across her chest that suggested she was a beauty pageant winner. She was quite obese and seemed to have trouble walking. She carried a large green trash bag that looked like it carried all her worldly possessions. And she was singing Aretha Franklin's *Respect* in a loud voice but struggled with the spelling.

"Hi. I'm Josh and this is my first time in the park," he said trying to interrupt her song.

She stopped singing and glared at him. "Hey. Don't you understand what I'm singing here?! Give me some respect! That's R.E.S.E.P.T!" she scolded. Now get the hell out of my way."

"Well, this isn't going very well," thought Josh, "but I'll give it a couple more tries."

He spotted another young man a bit off the path on the grass next to a tree. The man was laying on the grass and frequently moving to look past the tree. He was dressed in camouflage pants, a green T-shirt, and brown hiking boots. He had a camouflage baseball cap pulled down over his head barely leaving room for his eyes to peer out.

Josh left the path and walked over near where the man was lying. "Hi. I'm Josh and this is my first time in the park," he said.

"Quiet – they'll hear you!" hissed the man. "Get down!" he whispered and grabbed Josh's wrist pulling him down on the grass.

"Whaaa -? Who?" asked Josh as he landed on the ground.

"They're over there and they have guns!" whispered the man. "If they see us, we're dead."

"You see people in the park with guns?" asked Josh with appropriate concern. "They're here in the park?"

"What *park* you talking 'bout, buddy? They's holed up in that building just over there. Them A-rabs be shooting at us if we're not quiet!"

Josh quickly realized that this man and he did not share the same perception of reality and that he would not be having further useful conversation. "I'm going to flank them and try to flush them out. You keep watch," he suggested then got up and moved away.

"This is not working at all," thought Josh. It was about time to give up and return to the office. "One more try and that's it," he said to himself.

A little further on, Josh saw what appeared to be a woman sitting alone on a park bench feeding pigeons. "She looks harmless and maybe we could have a conversation."

As he approached, he saw more clearly that she was dressed in a dark gray overcoat with a torn right sleeve. She was wearing an old pair of Reeboks with a hole in the right sole. She had a bright red scarf wrapped loosely around the turned-up collar of the coat. "Strange attire for this time of year," thought Josh. He also noticed that she seemed to be mumbling to herself. All the signals indicated "Leave me alone." But he thought, "I said I'd give it one more try." So, he sat down on the bench not too near her and said, "Hi. I'm Josh and this is my first time in the park."

It was as if he wasn't even there. She just kept on mumbling and tossing breadcrumbs to a few pigeons. The pigeons for their part also seemed to ignore him, except for one that kept looking at him and slightly cocking its head.

After a little over a minute when it seemed the woman was just going to ignore him, Josh was frustrated and getting angry at himself for having wasted his time. He considered, "I thought finally getting out from under my mother's thumb and going to a park would be a liberating experience. This has been a total bust."

Just then the pigeon who had cocked its head walked over and pooped on his shoe.

"Damn it!" yelled Josh. "I've got enough shit going on in my life. I don't need the real thing. Damn you bird! And damn everyone in this park!" And Josh started to get up angrily to return to work.

The woman on the bench, Corrine Randall, reached out and grabbed his arm and said, "Stop. You have been chosen."

Chapter 5

Chosen

"What the hell do you mean I've been chosen? Chosen for what!?" Josh was getting more and more agitated by the moment and had pulled out his handkerchief to wipe the poop off his shoe.

Calmly, Corrine replied, "The dropping on your shoe is a message. Commander has selected you to take his wisdom to the world."

"What are you talking about?" shouted Josh. "Who's Commander? What message?" And further, "I came to this park today hoping for some closure and clarity for my life." And speaking faster, "I've just tried to say hello and have been ignored. Some man tried to sell me drugs. A crazy lady sang at me and couldn't spell. And someone tried to drag me into some imaginary battle he was still fighting. Now you – sitting here and mumbling, throwing breadcrumbs to pigeons, tell me that damn bird just crapped on my shoe to indicate I've been selected to take some message to the world!" He stood up and started to walk away.

But Corrine, again reached out and lightly touched his arm. She looked him in the eye and in a calm voice, "Please sit back down. This is important and I'll tell you everything." Her look was so intelligent, yet intense and forceful, he found himself sitting back down as much from embarrassment over his outburst as from curiosity. Given the other people he'd encountered, he thought she was just another crazy person, maybe with mental health issues, but for some reason he was also drawn to her and willing to listen, at least for a few moments.

"Okay. You seem a bit off, but not dangerous. I'll give you a moment to tell me what this is all about."

"It's a fairly long story and it will probably affirm your thoughts that I may be crazy. But everything I'm about to tell you is the absolute truth. And I will tell it to you because that is the message I got from Commander." Corrine continued, "I heard you say your name is Josh. My name is Corrine Randall, but now I go by Mary, and I am hiding out as a homeless bag lady because I fear for my life."

Josh stared at her thinking "This is going to be some story. Even though she said it's true, she looks like what I imagine a bag lady would look like. But she is so clear-eyed and articulate, something is off. I might as well listen." And aloud, "OK – let's hear why you're afraid for your life and hanging out like this."

Corrine – AKA Mary – told Josh the story of working at Flash, Flesh and Fantasy in Boston and overhearing her cop boyfriend, Jude, and the store owner talking about doing child pornography.

She told Josh how she'd heard Jude tell the store owner that he suspected she overheard them talking and that he would take care of it. Corrine took that to mean that she'd either keep quiet or he would kill her. "Not to be dramatic about it, but when I saw his police cruiser parked outside my apartment, I believed I had to escape. I went to a local Goodwill store and bought a few essentials with cash, then went to an ATM and withdrew all the meager funds I had." She exhaled. Then, "Maybe I was too paranoid and overthinking it, but I felt I was in danger and had to get away before he could find me."

She continued, "Having watched too many cop shows on TV, I believed I had to be careful not to leave a traceable trail. So, I avoided all public transportation and caught rides with good Samaritans. Eventually, I hitchhiked over many days not knowing where I was going and ended up here in Chicago. I was dropped off at this park by a couple nurses from Northwestern Hospital in March. As I walked around, I observed a number of people who seemed a bit odd carrying stuff in grocery carts, plastic trash bags, and small rolling suitcases. I figured they were almost invisible, so I decided to become like them."

"OK," responded Josh. "And I assume you fear Jude and his people are still after you, so you have to keep up this ruse even though it's been several weeks and you're over 1000 miles away." He made it sound more like a statement than a question to show he was listening but continued to wonder what this was all about.

As she nodded Josh said trying not to rush or be judgmental, "Keep going. What else?"

"Once I'd made my decision to stay, I had to gather some items to be convincing. Across Michigan Avenue behind some stores, I found this damaged pushcart and was able to fix the wheels a bit so I could push or pull it. I started gathering items from dumpsters including the clothes you see me wearing. I found cardboard and plastic trash bags that I used as bedding and protection from the weather. The workers at the coffee shop and the bakery often put out day-old food in the alley to be picked over by homeless people before the trash collectors picked it up. Over the weeks I collected enough of other peoples' throw-aways that I've been able to get by OK. At times when I'm sitting on a park bench, some kind person will stop and give me a sandwich or a bottle of water. I also got a blanket and then a sleeping bag. It brings me some gladness to witness the charity of some people."

Josh found himself being impressed by her inventiveness and resilience. She had by necessity become a survivor. "So, did you have any problems adapting to these circumstances?"

"There have been numerous challenges," she replied. "I've witnessed a number of muggings and assaults on other homeless people. I stay away from all of that as much as I can. I found an old bicycle chain that I wrap around my cart and leg at night so if someone tried to steal my stuff, it would wake me. I rarely go to shelters, mostly for food or to get out of bad weather, but they want to know my name and to keep track of me for further help. I tell them I'm Mary and no last name. Some places, but not all, will accept that for one night." She continued, "But my biggest problem has been with police. They patrol the parks to ensure safety and I've seen them haul away some people. Whenever they have approached me, I am quiet and polite but hide my speaking capabilities. They just tell me the laws and make sure I move along. I don't make trouble, and they have enough other things to deal with. At least so far, it's working."

Josh found himself getting drawn into her narrative. "Well, I'm sorry to hear all this has happened to you and have to admit I'm impressed. But what does this have to do with the pigeons and my being chosen?"

Corrine continued, "Over the first few weeks, as I scavenged for food, I would often get day-old bread from behind the bakery. Whenever I scored, I brought it back to a bench in the park and shared it with the birds. I noticed that there were a few pigeons that seemed to find me wherever I settled. It sounds strange, but I felt they were intentionally watching for me and it was for more than food. There were a few in particular that always seemed to be there and I found myself talking to them and giving them names based on their behaviors or coloration. One in particular," and she pointed at the one who pooped on my shoe, "I named Commander. He has these white shoulder epaulets and acts like he's in charge. The others," and she pointed to each in turn, "are Princess, Peace and Goldie. But it's Commander who is clearly the leader."

"Interesting study of animal behavior," responded Josh, "but I'm still missing the message idea."

"Josh, thanks for listening to my story so far. You've been very patient and kind," said Corrine. "But now things will get really strange and hard to believe. Do you want me to continue?"

"I'm intrigued," Josh replied. "As the saying goes, 'In for a penny, in for a pound.' I'm curious as to how the next part of the story goes and where I might fit in."

"OK. So as the weeks went on and I got, shall I say – more connected – to the pigeons, I noticed Commander often looking at me as if he was trying to communicate. When he noticed I was paying attention, he would do a little dance and drop his poop in various patterns. It seemed very intentional and intelligent. The more I watched over several days, I began to sense meaning in his droppings." Corrine paused and looked Josh in the eyes to see if he was believing this. He seemed to be.

"Then, and this is the woo-woo part, I got the sense of hearing a voice in my head. It was as if Commander was talking directly to my mind. What I heard, if that's the right word, is a story from Commander's point of view. It seems that pigeons first evolved about 34 million years ago and were first – as we call it – domesticated about 10,000 years ago, and more fervently about 5000 years ago in the Middle East, the Fertile Crecent. From what Commander 'tells' me, pigeons not only had great capabilities of geolocation – knowing where they were and returning to a home base – but also, get this, they had the capability of mental telepathy!"

Corrine paused again, carefully watching Josh's response. He simply nodded and motioned for her to continue.

"Again, according to Commander, way back then pigeons had a very deep understanding of the world and tried to communicate with humans and to give us a warning. As a species, humans had not evolved our abilities at mental telepathy so there was no interspecies communication. Over time, most pigeons lost their abilities to use telepathy, and most humans did not develop that skill. Fast forward to the present, according to Commander, only a few pigeons and a few humans are able to communicate telepathically, so most pigeons try to communicate through their droppings. They are trying to communicate this long-lost message that is of utmost importance to our kind. They hang around many government buildings and statues of important people, but we as humans just don't get the message, instead treating pigeons as vermin, as rats with wings. Fortunately, a few pigeons still try to communicate and have not given up."

Josh was staring at Corrine now with so much incredulity written all over his face, that it was hard for her to continue.

"But somehow, Commander has been able to communicate with me telepathically. I now know some of the basics of the lost message, but I can't go out in the world to share what I've learned. I'm deathly afraid Jude will find me."

"So what now?" Josh encouraged her.

"Commander deposited his droppings on your shoe to alert me that you are a good candidate to pass the message along to the masses. He says that I can be his intermediary to help you understand the message until, and if, you can ever communicate with him directly. This is why you have been chosen."

Chapter 6

The Message

Josh studied Corrine looking for any signs of deception, or even playfulness. All he saw was sincerity, and perhaps a little hopefulness. He decided to give her the benefit of the doubt, at least for now.

In a serious voice, "So, what is the message that so important that it needs to get out in the world and needs someone to spread the word?"

"From what I understand so far," replied Corrine, "the message is fairly straightforward but has a lot of history to back it up with examples and details." She paused, waiting to see if Josh would want to continue. She sensed that he had to ask for more rather than having it just laid out for him. She didn't want to make it too easy to reject, especially since on its surface, it wasn't very inspiring.

Josh pushed, "So tell me more. Give me some data." He felt a little more sure of himself using jargon from his own field of expertise.

"Well, as I understand it from Commander, through much of our shared history, pigeons have observed humans evolving a practice of trying to control the world around them. Perhaps I'm oversimplifying it, but he gave me examples of early humans struggling like the rest of the animals to get food just for survival. Plants were fairly easy because they were just there. But when it came to capturing animals for food, it was much harder. They learned to use sticks, bones and rocks as tools, often shaping them to be sharper or more efficient for hunting or protecting themselves from other predators and each other. Humans found ways to work together and often hunted in packs like other predators. They found ways to communicate with others in the pack to facilitate their efforts. Grunts, hand signals and so on proved useful in cornering their prey."

"But, as the pigeons noted, they then did something not seen in other species. They had developed concepts of time – not just the present and a bit of the past, but also a future. They began communicating about possibilities. Even before they went on a hunt, they communicated about what they were hunting and how to approach the task. They drew images in the dirt, scratched on rocks, and even in the caves that they used as shelters and meeting places. Even more, they started moving rhythmically and making sounds at different pitches to get ready for the hunt or after the hunt, to tell stories about their successes or failures. These, shall we call them 'rituals', were told over and over and shared with the young ones in their group. The stories in words, pictures, movement, and music were often enhanced to highlight certain actions or individuals."

She paused to see if Josh was following.

"Yes," Josh nodded. "It's a bit overly simplified, but most people today recognize those patterns of behavior of our ancestors, and even today. Things happen. We tell ourselves stories about them using words, pictures, possibly movement and music and pass the stories along to others. That's how we build our understanding of history and culture. So, what's the problem?"

"The problem, as you call it, again according to Commander, is that over time with the continual telling of these stories, they come to be seen as the way things actually are and we ignore how they've been embellished. And we take actions that demonstrate that we believe these things to be true."

"So what?" remarked Josh incredulously. "That's how we continue to learn and grow and evolve."

"True enough," said Corrine. "But, again according to Commander, we've come to the point where believing embellished truths, possibly falsehoods, have led to behaviors acting on those beliefs that are significantly dangerous to humans, other creatures, and the entire planet. We are destroying our collective home in part because we are acting on false stories."

"So the message is what…?" Josh asked.

Corrine took and breath and calmly related, "Don't obscure simple truth."

"'Don't obscure simple truth'!" Josh almost shouted. "'Don't obscure simple truth'!" He repeated. You've got to be kidding me. All this important message passed down by pigeons through the ages boils down to 'DON'T OBSCURE SIMPLE TRUTH'?!"

At this point, Commander who'd been standing several feet away from Corrine and Josh flapped his wings and took a little hop over to Josh and once again left a dropping – or should we say message – on his other shoe.

"Damn it!" Josh swore. Then, "I'm sorry, Corrine. I don't usually curse, but this is a bit much. You're telling me all this is coming from this pigeon – Commander – and that someone has to go out in the world and tell people 'Don't obscure simple truth'. It's ridiculous!" And Josh again started to get up, feeling disgusted and that he'd wasted his time and his opportunity for healing by being in the park.

And again, Corrine reached out and touched his arm. "Do you want to know what Commander just said?"

"Not really, but what?"

"He said you should examine your own response to this message. It's a different story than the one you tell yourself – about what you believe is real. Perhaps it is a way you obscure your simple truth."

Josh paused. He looked around and looked long and hard at Commander who was now a few feet away with his head cocked. He seemed to be asking Josh what he was thinking and what he was going to do about it.

"I've got to get back to work. This has been interesting and also a bit frustrating, to be honest." He paused again feeling like he had to say something further, perhaps even profound. "Have a nice day."

Chapter 7

Simple Truths

It had been three days since Josh had met Corrine in the park. He'd given a lot of thought to that experience, trying especially hard to ignore and dismiss the entire thing.

His curiosity led him to do a bit of research about pigeons. He learned that pigeons have strong cognitive abilities and communications skills. They can recognize individuals, even if the person changes their appearance. Their intelligence and ability to carry messages have been used throughout history, including in wartime. Two things particularly stood out in his research. First, some people believe that pigeons act as messengers between the mortal world and spiritual realms. And second, the genius behind many inventions, Nikola Tesla, had a deep connection with pigeons especially one in particular that he claimed he communicated with telepathically. "Maybe there is something to this story, after all," he thought.

According to Corrine, Commander had suggested that Josh examine his own reality, the stories he told himself consciously, and mostly unconsciously, about what was truth.

The memory hit hard. Josh had heard the story only one time when he was only 10 years old. It was so painful and troublesome that Josh had strongly rejected it to the point of forgetting it. About 5 years after his dad's deployment and death, his mom, Mary, told him about the circumstances of his birth. She'd been dating Joe Carpenter for a few months, but they had not been physically intimate. Mary and her best friend Angela had gone to a party. Someone had spiked their drinks with Rohypnol. Mary had no recollections from that night other than having awakened late the following morning and feeling achy all over her body, especially between her legs. A couple weeks later, realizing her period was late, a drugstore test showed she was pregnant. When he learned that she was pregnant, even though he knew he was not the father, Joe asked Mary to marry him so the child would have a man in his life. For Josh, Joe Carpenter had always been his dad even if he was not his biological father.

As this memory flooded into his consciousness, Josh understood that he had obscured a simple and very significant truth about himself. Maybe there was something to Commander's message after all.

Josh used his work computers and skills with artificial intelligence to ask, "What are some examples of simple truths?" The responses were not unexpected and included such things as:

- We all need love and connection.

- Change is constant.
- Actions have consequences.
- We are all mortal.
- Kindness matters.
- The present moment is all we have.
- Happiness comes from within.
- What you focus on grows.
- Nobody is perfect.
- Time is precious.
- Honesty builds trust.
- Hard work pays off.
- Life is unpredictable.
- Forgiveness frees you.
- You can't please everyone.
- Learning never stops.
- Gratitude brings joy.
- Life is what you make it.

As Josh read through these responses he thought, "I can see these statements are great concepts and most people would likely agree with this list. I also can imagine at least some people – skeptics and cynics – myself among them who might say 'Yes, but…' and follow with exceptions to these guidelines." He continued thinking, "Perhaps the exceptions arise out of people obscuring these simple truths."

So, Josh went further and directed his AI program to give examples of what might obscure simple truths. Here again, the generated list was not that surprising:

- Complexity and overthinking
- Emotions
- Ego and bias
- Cultural or societal influences

- Noise and distractions
- Denial and resistance
- Misinformation
- Fear of vulnerability
- Lack of mindfulness
- Overattachment to control

"Again," Josh thought, "these are still very basic generalizations." His next queries asked for specific historical examples. "Now we're getting interesting," thought Josh as he looked over the new list. "I can see where some of these 'truths' were obscured and how the revisions have affected our perceptions and behaviors in the current world." His thinking continued. "There may be something to this message from the pigeons after all. I'm curious enough to find Corrine and Commander to see if this is the kind of stuff we're talking about and why it's so important to take the message out into the world."

He went down to the deli on the lower floor of the Aon Center and bought a couple sandwiches, some fruit and a couple bottles of water. Again, as he crossed Randolph Street and went into the park, he noted that he had a very different purpose this time. Whereas before he wanted to recognize the passing of his mother and celebrate his liberation with a walk in the park, this time he was determined to learn more about this message and the implications it might hold for his life going forward.

He walked fairly quickly passing a few people with little more than a nod. He was on a mission and would not be distracted. He neared the bench where a few days before he had encountered Corrine and the pigeons. She was not there. Josh started to panic. "Did I blow it by dismissing their ideas when we were together? If this message is so important to humanity, have I caused a problem by not accepting that I was chosen to spread the word?" Self-doubt turned toward self- criticism. Then he remembered that Corrine said she moved around to different locations in the park to discourage the authorities from picking her up for loitering.

Re-energized, he started walking through the park, moving westward and scanning bench after bench. After about 10 minutes he spotted her on the side of the walkway on the east side of Michigan Avenue across from the Cultural Center. He could hardly believe how relieved he felt to have spotted her.

As Josh approached, he noticed she was again surrounded by pigeons as she fed them. Commander, Goldie, Princess, and Peace were among them obviously having found her in her new location just as Josh had. He also noticed there were a few people scattered not far from her waiting at the bus stop on Michigan Avenue or waiting to cross at the light. There was also a Chicago patrolman stationed on horseback standing along the sidewalk overseeing all the activity.

"Hi Corrine. I …"

"Shush!" she whispered loudly and gestured for him to be quiet. "They might hear you. And my name is Mary now." She furtively glanced at the policeman and pedestrians to assure herself that no one had taken notice.

Josh also looked about and felt they were secure. He said, "I brought you a sandwich, some fruit and water. I'd like to talk some more."

Corrine/Mary said, "You can give me what you brought and act like a good Samaritan, but we can't talk here." She reached out to accept the bag he'd brought and more loudly, just mumbled her thanks. Then quietly, "We can't be seen talking here. Too many people. Go over toward the steps leading up to the Bean and find a bench near the skating rink. I'll eat what you brought me then make my way over and find you."

Josh thought she was being a bit paranoid, but he really wanted to talk with her. He wondered if he moved away whether she – and Commander – would really follow.

Josh found a bench slightly off the path near where she'd suggested. He settled onto the bench and ate his own sandwich and apple. About 10 minutes later, he noticed Corrine/Mary pushing her broken roller cart along the walkway not far from him. She approached and sat down on the same bench, positioning her cart between them to make it seem like they weren't together. Almost immediately, several pigeons landed nearby and looked at her expectantly. She had eaten the meat and cheese but had saved the bread slices. She began pulling off little chunks and feeding them to the birds. Josh noticed Commander was right there with the rest of them but was looking more at Josh and did not seem as interested in the bread.

Before Josh could say anything, Corrinne not looking at him said, "You must call me Mary. You must think of me as Mary. That is who I am now." She went on. "Yesterday I was digging through some trash thrown out behind an office building. Among the papers I found a page from a Word-A-Day calendar. That word was 'pentimento'. The calendar page definition was 'a change made by the artist during the subsequent paint layer'. The example given was of Picasso's The Old Guitarist." She paused. "What people see now is the latest representation of me, not any of the earlier versions. What is now true of me. I am Mary. Corrine is no longer seen."

Josh nodded and replied, also not looking directly at her, "I get it. Mary is who you are and who you will be."

They sat quietly sharing a bench not looking at each other and with a broken cart between them.

After several minutes, Josh said, "I've been thinking about what you told me Commander said and how he questioned whether I might be deceiving myself about what I believe is true. I found it to be an intriguing question that I just couldn't let go. I re-examined my own life and realized I had a large and important blind spot about my past. I'd been obscuring an important truth about who I am." He chose not to disclose what he'd realized, but only said, "It made me want to know more about simple truths and ways we might hide or disguise them."

Josh went on to talk about how that encouraged him to do more. "So, I used my skills in data analysis and artificial intelligence and got a long list of what many people might consider simple truths. The sceptic in me could come up with lots of exceptions to each one. Then I asked what might cause any of these truths to be obscured. Again, the list of responses was pretty straightforward." Josh shared a few examples with Mary.

In the next moment, Commander hopped over and left another dropping on Josh's shoe. This time, instead of being disgusted, Josh asked, "What did he say?"

"Commander said … and it seem like he was almost shouting … he said, 'MAINLY HARMLESS.' By that, I take it he means those simple truths and ways they are obscured are not that important."

Josh agreed. "That's what I thought as well. But thinking there must be something more important otherwise Commander wouldn't be as concerned, I then asked for examples that might illustrate how simple truths have been obscured throughout human history. The response to that query got me really thinking about Commander's message and why it might be important to spread the word."

Mary responded that Commander is hopeful that Josh may now understand the message and why it is significant. She asked, "What's an example that made you start to think there might be something significant?"

"There were so many. And it's not just the truth that was obscured, but the personal and societal reaction to each one. Behaviors changed and some are responsible for the ways some people think and act today. I dug deeper into the history of theories about the structure of the universe. Early humans looked at the heavens and the layout of the visible stars. They imagined lines connecting some stars and drew pictures of constellations. They told each other stories about what the constellations meant and the power and influence they had over our lives on Earth. Even today there are some people who believe that the ways people act are determined by which constellation was in the sky at the time of their birth."

Josh went on. "As I considered this, I also thought about the actual structure of our solar system. The position of the sun and the motions of the planets – the data input as it were – was the same for everyone although the ability to observe and mathematically track the movements improved over time. However, there were many different theories based on the data even as far back as 5000 years ago, in ancient China, Persia, Greece and Rome. And then Copernicus in the early 1500s. By the 17th century, most people believed that the Earth was the center of the Universe – the geocentric model. That the sun and all the other planets revolved around the Earth. And through observation and mathematics they could prove it."

"Yeah," interjected Mary. "I learned in school about how Galileo following on the work of Copernicus and others, showed a different model that had the sun as the center of our solar system."

"Yes, and for our purposes," continued Josh, "it was the Catholic Church that upheld the idea of geocentrism because it supported their entrenched ideas about the creation of the universe and mankind's place in it. Earth *had* to be the center of everything. They arrested and tried Galileo for his heliocentric ideas. Under pressure, Galileo recanted. The simple truth, at least as we now know it, is that the Earth revolves around the sun. People in power didn't want that truth to be known so they controlled the flow of information." Josh paused and took a breath. "And now there are other truths that get obscured and where the flow of information is controlled to support those in power."

"So," responded Mary, "that sounds like it's not only about what is true, but how people respond to it, embracing it or covering it up."

"Absolutely," Josh replied excitedly. "The message not to obscure simple truth must mean that we need to expose the ways significant truths have been manipulated for whatever reason by those in power. And that by making people aware of those manipulations, everyone can understand the real truths."

Commander was watching and listening to the conversation. He bobbed his head rapidly then strutted around near their feet and deposited a large dollop of his digested food.

Mary exclaimed, "Commander says we're on the right path. That it's not necessarily the specific truth to be concerned about, but how we as humans have adopted various explanations and used our explanations to influence others, often with serious ramifications for the larger society and the planet."

Josh looked at Commander's droppings and those of some of the other nearby pigeons. "You got all that from those droppings?" he asked incredulously. "That's an awful lot to consider given the source." He chuckled. "But it does make sense when I think of it. The message, 'Don't obscure simple truth' is more about the obfuscation and manipulation of explanations than about the truths themselves." Josh paused, then asked, "Now what?"

Mary looked at Josh directly in his eyes for the first time since they'd been together today. "I believe you need to find a way to get the word out, to share the message and your understanding of its importance."

Josh looked back at her having gone a bit pale. "Now that I better understand the message and why it is important, I'm a bit flummoxed. What needs to happen? And why me? I've got my work and other things to do. I didn't sign up for this!" Josh was starting to back away from taking action. Self-doubt was diving him away from this calling.

"Mary, you're the one who can read the droppings and hear Commander's voice in your head. You should be the one to take this message to people, not me," he protested.

"Josh, you know why I can't do that. If I am seen, Jude and his fellow cops will find me, and I'll be killed. Also, even in these times, the fact that I am a woman means people won't listen to me as well as they would to a man." She paused. "And Commander has chosen you!"

"But if I go out there and start telling people they are mistaken and being manipulated by powerful people and institutions that want to control what they think and how they act, *my* life will be in danger!"

Josh was almost shouting as his fear of following through on this assignment became clearer.

Just then, Commander flitted over to Josh, bobbed his head then cocked it slightly over his right shoulder, then straightened up and bobbed his head a bit more.

"He looks like he's encouraging you to do this," suggested Mary. "And he says he will be with you as you go on this journey you are called to take."

"Well, he and you wouldn't be the ones in danger. I have to think about this." Josh stood up and started to walk back to his day job. He turned slightly and said, "Have a nice day."

Chapter 8

Accepting the Mission

For the next week Josh tried to minimize the entire experience with Mary and Commander and the other pigeons. He laughed at himself for going as far as he had. He thought about how ridiculous the entire idea was that he'd almost been suckered into. "Pigeons communicating with humans through their droppings or some being able to use mental telepathy. And all because of some important message that they thought humanity needed to understand: 'Don't obscure simple truth'. And, this bag lady, Corrine, who now calls herself Mary. Clearly she has some mental problems and believes her life is in danger. What a big joke on me."

Then, Josh started to notice things in his experiences. They had always been there, but now they grabbed his attention.

The first thing he noticed as he was paying a different kind of attention was some of the people riding the Green Line after work as he was headed home. There was the usual mix of business commuters, most with their attention focused on their phone, a book or newspaper, or taking a nap. There was a scattering of tourists who were returning from their adventures exploring in the Loop. And there was the occasional beggar going up and down the aisles asking for any small monetary contribution someone might choose to make. He'd always ignored those people or sometimes looked at them and smiled. But today he noted that some would actually say something to a person who gave them some change or a dollar bill. He listened to the beggar say "Thank you" or "Bless you". As one in particular clothed in not much more than torn jeans and rags approached, he looked Josh in the eyes. Instead of asking for spare change, he quietly said, "I have been appointed to help people learn about the truths of gratitude, generosity, and grace."

Josh was suddenly taken aback. Had he heard correctly? This guy mentioned he'd been appointed, and it had something to do with truths. Was he connected to the pigeons somehow? Before Josh could respond, his train pulled into the stop at Cicero and the beggar exited. As he did so, he turned back into the car and said to no one in particular, "Have a nice day."

The next morning, as Josh walked from his stop at State and Lake and up Randolph Street, he was aware that there seemed to be more pigeons around. And where there were pigeons, there were droppings. Most people avoided the mess, some even cursing the vermin and their filth. Josh wondered what it was the pigeons were trying to communicate.

Then, at work, talking with John about some of their projects on data collection and analysis related to climate change, he realized he was going beyond the data and was thinking about the various implications of how people were interpreting the exact same data but telling different stories to explain what it all meant. He thought about who was making the explanations and how they might be choosing what to say and how to influence beliefs and behaviors. Some people and institutions were focused on the real and potential damage human actions were having on the health of the planet. Some of those explanations predicted doomsday scenarios where we would either destroy the planet or the planet would fight back and destroy humankind. Some were explaining that the data showed that the greenhouse effects of burning fossil fuels were overstated. They emphasized that a couple of degrees of temperature change had happened numerous times throughout the Earth's history, and we've survived them all. Some even suggested that the effects on the environment were a further encouragement to space exploration, to push humans to explore and settle on other planets. Even with everyone looking at the same data, different people and institutions had their own ways of suggesting what the problems were and what to do about them. Politicians, religious leaders, and environmentalists all had their own take on it. And only some of those ideas made it into popular media and into the classrooms teaching our students about the effects of climate change.

It all seemed to Josh to be similar to the contrasting theories between geocentric and heliocentric models of the solar system, but much more immediate and significant.

Josh was getting a sense that as reluctant and dismissive as he was about being chosen to spread the message to the world, something was happening in his psyche that wouldn't let him stop thinking about it. He thought to himself, "It's like thinking about buying a specific model and color of car. I hadn't noticed them much before, but now I'm seeing them everywhere." He recalled from some of his college coursework that this is known as the frequency illusion, or the Baader- Meinhof phenomenon, and it occurs through two psychological processes: selective attention and confirmation bias. Selective attention means you're hyper-attuned to seeing things you're thinking about while confirmation bias validates that what you're noticing is what's actually going on.

In any case, Josh felt that he needed to examine this more carefully and that would require him returning to the park and talking with Mary, and possibly Commander.

About 11:30 that morning, he again went to the deli in the basement of the AON Center and bought sandwiches and water for himself and Mary. He realized he was now thinking of her more as Mary than Corrine and wondered if that was another indication that he was moving toward taking on this challenge. As almost an afterthought, he asked the counterperson if they had any day-old bread that he could have to feed the pigeons. It was yet another reinforcement of his growing buy-in.

As he crossed Randolph Street and entered the park, he noted that there were many people from various office buildings entering and walking around in the park. "I wonder if any of these people have communicated with the pigeons or been chosen for any tasks like the rider on the train," he considered. "Or, like Thoreau's mass of men, are they leading lives of quiet desperation – or rather, acceptance of what they are told are the truths without questioning the veracity and implications of selective understanding or manipulation?"

Josh looked at the various places he had encountered Mary previously, but she was nowhere to be seen. He walked further south into Millennium Park to the southern end of the Great Lawn near the west end of the BP Pedestrian Bridge. He spotted Mary spread out on a grassy area as if she were having a picnic. The only food he saw was a few pieces of bread that she was tossing out to the surrounding pigeons. He noted that Commander was among the flock.

"Hi Mary," he said as he approached her. "I walked all over the park looking for you and am glad I found you." He paused. "I've brought you a sandwich and some water. And look, I even thought to get some day-old bread to share with our friends."

Mary looked at Josh with a Mona Lisa smile. She seemed most taken by the bread and Josh's referral to the pigeons as "our friends". "It's good to see you Josh. Come sit with me."

Josh squatted down and sat a couple feet away from Mary conscious about not giving an onlooker the wrong impression of their relationship. Commander was studying Josh, especially the bread he'd brought. Josh sensed that Commander was almost smiling at him and saying, "Thank you". He got the further sense that Commander was "talking" to him and was glad he came back.

Josh told Mary about some of the unusual experiences he'd had: the man on the train, the large number of pigeons and their droppings, and the conversation with his co-worker, John, about the climate research data and its implications and manipulations depending on the individual or institution that was interpreting the data and suggesting its meaning. Mary listened and nodded as he talked. But, thought Josh, more interesting was how Commander seemed to be listening and nodding as well.

Then Commander deposited another large dropping between the two of them. "Oh my," Mary said, studying the dropping. "Commander says you are ready to start to take the message out into the world."

"And how does Commander suggest I do that?" Josh asked, starting to wonder again if this was real.

"Tomorrow at 12:45 come back to this area and go into Lurie Garden. The entrance is just over there," she said nodding her head slightly in a direction over Josh's left shoulder. When there, you will find someone who will help you spread the word." Mary continued. "Commander says he will be watching and helping guide you."

Josh was intrigued but also very nervous. He'd read about that garden and knew it to be crowded with wildflowers, prairie grasses, and flowering bushes. The thought of all those flowers and scents brought him right back to his 5-year-old self and the trauma suffered as his mother had thought Josh was teasing her about her anosmia. The emotions were staggering. "Couldn't I go somewhere else? Talk to someone else? There are too many flowers in the garden." Josh pleaded.

"No," replied Mary. "You told me your history and relationship with parks and especially with flowers. I think it must be that you have to face that memory and work through it to honestly share the message that Commander has chosen you for."

Josh looked at Commander who was watching him and bobbing his head up and down.

"Uh, OK then. I'll see you tomorrow at 12:45."

"I may not be here at that time. I think this is a mission for you to undertake with just Commander at your side. I would be a distraction, especially in the garden, looking like I am."

Josh sighed heavily. "Ok. I understand. I'll be here with Commander."

Josh got up and began the half-mile walk back to his office wondering what he'd gotten himself into.

Chapter 9

Lurie Garden

The next morning as Josh walked to the Green Line station and again on the train, he noticed several of what he used to think of as homeless people and beggars. Most of them didn't make eye contact with him or anyone else. They just held out the cup or perhaps a piece of cardboard with scrawling like, "Please Help. Homeless Vet" or "Willing to work" even "Help me feed my 2 kids." He still felt uncomfortable looking at them and wondered how true their pleadings were. But he figured they were mainly harmless and didn't give them much more thought. He did notice that a few fellow commuters did give some of these people a little money, or a bottle of water, or at least said hello. Josh couldn't help but wonder if that was the right thing to do. He'd heard that giving handouts just reinforced these begging behaviors and kept people in their destitute conditions.

However, once again, there was one person on the train, a different person today. He approached people, most of whom leaned away from his foul odor or didn't pay any attention hoping he'd just go away. He had no sign or cup but mumbled something about having been appointed to tell people something important. When he approached Josh, their eyes met, and Josh asked what it was he had to say. The man was startled that he'd gotten a response and didn't seem to know what was so important. Josh asked, "Is it a message?"

"Yeh! Yeh!" The man excitedly replied. Then he paused and looked bewildered. "But... don't remember what. It's important though. Someone's got to tell it."

The man continued to act more and more agitated. He'd found someone who might listen, but he didn't know what to say. His eyes darted around in the car and other passengers were looking at him. His discomfort seemed to increase, and he moved toward the exit. As they pulled into the station at Pulaski, he glanced around again and jumped out on the platform. Then he twisted around, looked straight at Josh and said, "Have a nice day." Then disappeared just as the train started to move out of the station.

By the time Josh got off at State and walked up Randolph to his office in the Aon Center, he had convinced himself that this was another sign and meant directly for him. His "nice day" would include going to Lurie Garden to start spreading the message somehow. He wasn't sure what that might look like, but he felt confident that Commander would somehow guide him on what to do and whom to talk to.

At 12 noon Josh left his office and decided to skip lunch. He was so nervous he didn't think he could keep it down. As he walked past the Pritzker Band Shell and through the lawn under the trellis he kept an eye out for Mary. But just as promised, she was nowhere to be seen. This was on him. As he neared the northern entrance to Lurie Garden, his heart was beating so hard in his chest that he thought he might have a heart attack. He wasn't sure if his anxiety was because he'd be surrounded by so many flowers or because of his new mission to spread the message not to obscure simple truth. Probably it was both.

He noticed a few pigeons near the entrance. Commander was among them. Josh felt a sense of comfort, a sense of purpose. He felt support, yes even love, coming from Commander and was able to gain confidence to cross the threshold.

Once inside the garden, he was almost surprised at its beauty. It was not scary. It was laid out with multiple walking paths winding their way through a full palette of color and scents. Every few feet he saw little signs stuck in the ground identifying the plants with their scientific name and common name. He noticed several people, volunteers he assumed, working in various areas of the garden, pruning plants and bushes, transplanting flowers, pulling weeds, and so much more. There were many people, some businesspeople on lunch breaks, some visitors who just wanted to experience the beauty and serenity of the garden. He realized his breathing had slowed, his heart palpitations were gone, and he was just feeling calm as he strolled about.

After about 10 minutes walking around in the garden, he remembered that he was here for a purpose. He was supposed to meet someone and begin to spread the message. He looked around, but Commander wasn't anywhere in sight. He felt that he'd been abandoned and started to get anxious again.

Just then, a young man dressed in clean blue jeans, work boots and a light blue work shirt approached. He had a badge on his shirt identifying him as Peter Fisher and as a park employee. He was carrying a smart phone in his hand. "Hi there, sir. Would you mind talking with me for a few minutes?"

Josh was annoyed. He was supposed to be talking with someone as directed by Commander, but here he was being waylaid by a Park Services employee. A bit shortly he said, "I'm actually on a bit of a mission and don't want to take time talk to you."

Peter continued almost as if he hadn't heard and had a prepared speech. "I am a Chicago Park District employee and have been tasked with speaking to people who visit Lurie Garden to get a sense of why they come, what they value. I'm a media specialist and create a podcast called Experiences in the Garden of what I learn from the people I talk to. It's my job to hear what people like you have to say and then spread the word. So, this will only take a couple minutes." Then pulling up his cell phone app, he said, "Do you mind if I record this?"

Josh, although agitated, had been politely listening, actually waiting til the guy was done so he could say "No thank you" and go on with his task. But Peter's phrase, "to hear what people like you have to say and then spread the word" caught his attention. Was this another sign? Was this the person he was supposed to talk with to start to spread the message?

Josh looked about to see if there was anyone else who he might be intended to talk with. He also looked for but did not see Commander. But he had a sense. This was the beginning.

"Ok, I'll talk with you, and you can record it."

Peter was excited. "Thank you so much. Most people just tell me to go bother someone else. Some are rude. Some are polite and at least say, "Have a nice day." Thank you so much." He paused, then asked, "Would you tell me your name and what brings you to Lurie Garden today?"

With no hesitation, Josh said, "My name is Josh Carpenter and I'm here on a mission."

Peter was intrigued. "What's the mission?"

"I'm seeking simple truths. I want to understand some truths this garden holds and how we might be manipulating them for some alternate purpose."

"Sounds nefarious," Peter replied. I can't imagine anything in this garden that isn't exactly what it seems."

"You're probably right and this is just a ridiculous pursuit." He paused. "But let's see if we can come up with any example. I'm relatively ignorant about flowers and being here is almost overwhelming. Some of the flowers in here look familiar but I couldn't identify them if I had to. I appreciate that there are little signs near the plants that identify them." Josh pointed to a nearby identifier.

"Yes," said Peter. "Many people appreciate that we have signage that tells them what they are looking at."

"Well," said Josh, "I noticed that most of the signs show at least two names."

"That's true. Every plant has a scientific name, its genus and species. That's the way that plant is known no matter where it is found in the world. Each scientific name is unique. The other name, or names, are what are known as common names. These are the names that, shall I say, non-scientists call the plant in a particular geographic area. That same plant may grow elsewhere and be given a different common name. It can get a bit confusing."

"Aha," exclaimed Josh. "So, the simple truth is the scientific name, the raw undisputed data. Everyone, at least botanists, would agree that that is the true name. So why are there different common names?"

"Well," said Peter warming to the discussion, "I am a trained and certified botanist, so you've come to the right person. Look at this plant here," said Peter pointing to a green plant with oval-shaped leaves that were about 7 inches long and 5 inches wide. The leaves were arranged in a rosette lying close to the ground. The leaves themselves had a ribbed texture with 5 veins that were parallel to each other. "As the identification marker says this is *Plantago major*. The common name shown is 'Broadleaf Plantain' and it's one of my favorites concerning common names."

Peter continued. "Sometimes it's simply known as the Greater Plantain to distinguish it from a smaller similar plant. Other names are Soldier's Herb and Healing Blade because it was often used for healing wounds and cuts. And one of my favorites is White Man's Footprint. This is what some indigenous North American groups named it because of how the plant spread in disturbed soil after European settlement."

"Peter, why do you think there are so many different names for the same plant?" Josh asked.

"Well, there are a number of reasons that I'm aware of. Some names are given because of how a plant looks – its color, shape or size. Some are named for the habitat in which they are found in a given region, like a dry soil or marshy area. Some names indicate their various uses as a medicine or for landscaping. And some, like

I mentioned with the Plantain, are given names by an indigenous group because of their impact on that specific group of people."

"This is fascinating," remarked Josh. "Everyone is looking at the same plant, but for their own reasons, they have different ways they commonly talk about it. And I'd guess that if a person or group knew it by a different common name than another person or group, they might have difficulty understanding what they are talking about, or even have disputes about who is right."

"Yes, that happens a lot," chuckled Peter. "The disputes have led to confusion, but as far as I know, no disagreement has come to blows."

"So," Josh thought out loud, "We have an example of obscuring a simple truth. But in these cases, they are mainly harmless."

They were each quiet for a few moments, each thinking about what they'd discussed.

Peter turned to Josh and said, "You know, I realize I've probably taken more of your time than I promised. But I found this conversation rather interesting." He paused, then continued. "You said you came to Lurie Garden on a mission. Tell me now, what is your mission?"

Josh took a deep breath. This was it. "I have come to give a message to humanity: 'Don't obscure simple truth'. I am looking for examples of where we have done that, intentionally or otherwise, and how it has affected our thought process, beliefs, and behaviors."

"Wow," responded Peter. "That sounds a bit profound. I hope our conversation helped you in some way."

"Indeed it did," smiled Josh. "You helped me understand that simple truths are just about everywhere we look and that we can very easily obscure the truths simply based on how we talk about them, how we give different names to the same things for various reasons." After a moment, he continued. "And it's not so much about what the truth is or how we've come up with various ways of describing it. Those are mainly harmless. It's the more significant truths that we describe and pass on to others that can lead to conflicts and disputes. I want to understand that more."

Peter looked at Josh for a moment with an intensity beyond their brief encounter. "I think you're on to something, Josh. I'm going to put some of this out in my podcast if that's OK. And I'd like to talk with you again and hear more about your mission and what you're learning."

Josh was slightly taken aback. He'd just been having an interesting conversation with a park employee and realized that he had, in fact, spread the message. And that the podcast could spread it even further. He was clearly on the journey now.

"I'd like that as well, Peter. I often walk through the park every few days around this time. I'd be happy to meet again and talk further."

Peter was clearly at least as excited as Josh. He said, "I'm here again next Thursday. I hope we can meet then. I'll watch for you. In the meantime, feel free to listen to my podcast," and handed Josh a business card with the podcast URL listed.

"Sounds like a plan," replied Josh. "I look forward to it."

As they started to move off in their separate directions, Peter called out, "Have a nice day."

Chapter 10

Common Names

As Josh exited the garden, he looked around for Commander. What he noticed was several park personnel and animal control workers trying to round up the large number of pigeons that had gathered.

Josh approached one of the workers. "What's going on? What's with all the pigeons?"

"We got several calls, complaints really. People who were trying to get into Lurie Garden were saying that a large flock of pigeons had gathered and was making a mess of the area with all their droppings. We were called in to capture them or shoo them away and to clean up the mess they'd made."

"Wow," said Josh. "When did this happen?"

"It seems to have started about 12:45. It's been going on about half an hour, but I think we're getting it under control now. The pigeons seem to be moving away on the own accord. I guess it worked, whatever we did."

"Well, good luck and thanks." Josh walked away from the area thinking, "Perhaps I wasn't abandoned after all."

A few minutes later he was passing by Cloud Gate, the art installation better known as the Bean. As he gazed at the shiny surface and its reflection of the city, his eye was drawn to a motion. He turned around and saw that the motion had been a pigeon flying by. It was Commander. The bird flew over to the east side of the plaza and landed on the corner of a bench. He seemed to stand tall and flutter his wings. He looked in Josh's direction and bobbed his head. Then he flew off to the east along the walkway to the pavilion.

Josh gathered that he was meant to follow and did so. About 50 feet down the path, he spotted Mary off to the side. Commander was nearby.

As he approached, Mary said, "Don't stop. People may be watching. Just walk on by." Then added, "It's started."

Josh was disappointed. He wanted to tell her – them – all about his experience in Lurie Garden meeting and talking with Peter, discussing the names given to plants and the connection to obscuring simple truth, even if it was mainly harmless. He wanted to tell them that Peter had been following closely and recorded the conversation for his podcast and they were going to meet again on Thursday to continue their conversation.

But Mary and Commander seemed to ignore him. They either were not interested or, he hesitated, they already knew. Maybe that's why all those other pigeons were clustered about. They were witnessing the exchange and perhaps passing it along to Commander, who then passed it along to Mary.

Josh quietly accepted that he would not be speaking with Mary and Commander today. He was more focused on what he'd shared with Peter and they were going to continue to talk on Thursday. He was also excited that Peter was making a podcast and he'd be a part of it. He wondered what Peter would say and who might be listening.

Almost as an afterthought, he realized he'd spent close to half an hour inside a space heavily populated with all sorts of flowers and had not been bothered by the colors and smells. If he was honest about it, he'd actually enjoyed the experience, and the trauma suffered at the hands of his mother never occurred to him once he was a few feet inside the garden. It was truly liberating and healing.

As he walked back to his office and the work that awaited him, he thought more about what Peter had said about the common names of *Plantago major*. "One of my favorites is White Man's Footprint. This is what some indigenous North American groups named it because of how the plant spread in disturbed soil after European settlement."

Josh thought about what was included in that comment and how it related to a very significant truth that had been obscured by European settlers. He decided he wanted to learn more and talk further with Peter about his discoveries.

Chapter 11

Experiences in the Garden

"Simple truth: Indigenous peoples have inherent rights to their land, culture and autonomy." That's what came up on Josh's query the next morning. When Josh queried about how that truth has been obscured through history, there were countless examples. Most interesting to Josh, perhaps because of Peter's comment, were those related to native Americans – First Peoples of North America. The AI commentary went on to explain that simple truth was obscured in a number of ways.

First listed was colonialism, which rationalized exploitation and conquest based on the belief that it was "manifest destiny", that somehow it was meant to be, perhaps by divine right, that the colonists – invaders – were fated to take over the land and disrupt the beliefs and culture of the people living there. Some actions were taken using the argument that the colonists were intending to civilize the heathens. Because the indigenous people did not believe in the Christian God, they had to be converted or killed. The mostly white people whose roots were from Europe, also wanted more land for their own purposes as they moved westward. There were all kinds of justifications for the actions taken against the indigenous peoples including wars, the spread of disease, displacement efforts, and treaties that were not adhered to.

Another way the simple truth was obscured through history and into the present day revolved around economic factors. Some people prioritized land development over indigenous sovereignty. Whether for farming, ranching, industry, or places for non-Native people to live, many indigenous groups were confined to reservations or forcibly relocated further and further away. Today, it seems that many of those in power try to placate the impoverished reservations by allowing some sovereignty and the ability to build and run entertainment venues from which the native peoples can keep the profits.

Josh understood that his brief research had just uncovered the tip of an immense iceberg of human history relative to the incursion of one group of people into the territory, culture and beliefs of an indigenous population. Going back through recorded history – and even before - with the stories that had been passed down orally from generation to generation, there were patterns of behaviors that demonstrated some people and institutions push out natives or take over territory or work to convert belief systems to fit with the conquering people. Josh remembered some of his learning from his undergrad philosophy classes. "This is what was meant by 'might is right' as attributed to the Greek historian Thucydides in The History of the Peloponnesian War between Sparta and Athens in the 5th Century BCE. The strong do what they have the power to do and the weak accept what they have to accept. Another ancient Greek, Plato, referred to this in his dialogue called The Republic in having Socrates refute the statement, instead proposing that justice should prevail over power, that ethical and just principles should prevail over sheer strength or dominance.

"And," Josh continued to consider, "even in the world today, there are many people and institutions who seem to act based more on the sense that they have the power than that what they do is ethically just for all involved. The simple truth that indigenous peoples have inherent rights to their land, culture and autonomy has been and continues to be obscured in so many ways."

At this point, Josh wondered what Peter might have posted in his podcast. He pulled out the card Peter had given him and entered to address on his computer.

"Hi everyone and welcome to another episode of Experiences in the Garden. I'm your host, Peter Fischer, an employee of the Chicago Park District. My task has been to interview visitors to Lurie Garden to share their experiences with the wider public." He paused after his typical daily introduction. "Today, I want to share something a bit different from a very engaging conversation I had with Josh Carpenter yesterday. When I invited Josh to share why he was in the garden, he said (playing the voice recording), 'I am here on a mission.' (pause) 'I'm seeking simple truths.'"

Peter's voice continued. "I was intrigued. We went on to talk about the signage we put around the garden to identify the various plants. We clarified that every plant has a unique scientific name, its genus and species, no matter where it may have come from. Josh said he thought the scientific names might be considered as simple truths in that they were the same raw data that everyone agreed on. Then Josh asked me 'So why are there different common names?'"

The podcast went on. "I replied" (and Peter played a recording of his voice), 'Some names are given because of how a plant looks – its color, shape or size. Some are named for the habitat in which they are found in a given region, like a dry soil or marshy area. Some names indicate their various uses as a medicine or for landscaping. And some… are given names by an indigenous group because of their impact on that specific group of people.'"

"Then the conversation took a different turn than I've ever experienced. When I asked Josh to say more about his mission, he said, 'I have come to give a message to humanity: Don't obscure simple truth. I am looking for examples of where we have done that, intentionally or otherwise, and how it has affected our thought processes, beliefs, and behaviors.'"

"Whoa!" exclaimed Peter in his podcast. "'Don't obscure simple truth'. On the surface that sounded so simplistic and yet profound." Peter paused. "Josh and I talked about some examples referring to the signage in the garden. It didn't seem too nefarious. And then I heard his second thought. Of the examples we discussed about how simple truth had been obscured in some our naming practices, Josh said, 'in these cases, they are mainly harmless.'"

"Another big whoa for me! 'Mainly harmless!' I think Josh may be on to something, and it's about much more than the flowers in Lurie Garden. I'll be talking more with Josh about the meaning and impact of 'Don't obscure simple truth' and 'Mainly harmless' in the next few days. Tune back in to hear about Josh's thoughts on these two concepts."

"In the meantime, this is Peter Fischer coming to you with Experiences in the Garden. Tune in next week to hear more of this and other stories."

Josh turned off the podcast and thought to himself, "'Whoa' is right. The way Peter captured the essence of our conversation even helps me be clearer about what I'm doing. I have to think about what he and I will talk about now that I've heard how he puts it in his podcast."

Chapter 12

The *What?* Questions

Josh was very busy at work but found little snippets of time where he did further research and thinking about simple truths and how they'd been doctored over time by whoever or whatever had the power to tell the story to their own advantage. It was close to overwhelming to consider just a handful of topics, but he kept at it to see what else might arise in his thinking.

Thursday late morning he headed over to the park again hoping to see Mary and Commander before meeting with Peter. He scoured the park but found no sign of either of them or the other loyal following of pigeons. Finally, as 12:35 approached, he again made his way toward Lurie Garden to talk with Peter. Those feelings of abandonment arose again, and he questioned why he was left alone with this important mission. They had promised to be with him on this journey, but now that things were getting some traction, they were nowhere to be seen.

Josh was feeling a bit clearer on his mission and that Peter and his podcast were a part of it. Yes, Mary and Commander had started him on this path, but he was feeling more and more like the mission was his whether they were there to guide him or share in the journey.

As he passed through the north entrance to the garden, he spotted Peter a few paths away talking with another patron, his phone held to best capture their recorded voices. Josh didn't want to intrude so he approached slowly waiting to catch Peter's eye.

"Ah, there you are," exclaimed Peter. "The man of the hour." He gestured to the person he was talking with. "Josh, this is my brother, Andrew Fisher. He's always been supportive of my efforts at podcasting, and he listened to the latest episode about the two of us talking."

Andrew jumped in. "Yes, I found the description of your mission to be most intriguing and want to learn more. Would you mind if I joined you and Peter in today's conversation?"

Josh, though slightly taken aback, responded, "That's fine with me." And after a pause, looked at Peter and said, "I listened to your podcast as well. The way you captured our conversation and emphasized the two statements, 'Don't obscure simple truth' and 'Mainly harmless' helped me get even more clarity about my mission. Thank you."

Peter had turned on the voice recording app on his phone and gestured to show it was on. Josh nodded and continued. "My professional life involves analyzing big data and utilizing artificial intelligence to extract trends and themes. I did a little more research on simple truths and how they're obscured. It's fascinating to see how what might be a simple truth has been obscured by people and institutions for their own purposes." Josh went on to share some of what he'd been thinking about the AI-suggested truth that indigenous peoples have inherent rights to their land, culture and autonomy. Both Peter and Andrew offered examples of that truth being obscured throughout history in many places and cultures around the world, often by governments with their armies or religions with their evangelists.

"So, Josh, what are you thinking about all this and how does it fit with your mission?" asked Andrew.

"Well, first of all, it's humbling. With my professional skills and using AI, I can identify countless examples of simple truths being obscured for many reasons. But I'm at a bit of a loss what to do about it." He paused. "One idea that occurred to me was to go through the series of *What?* questions as I looked at the AI-generated reports I was getting."

Andrew held up his hand signaling Josh to wait a moment. "What are the *What?* questions?"

Josh explained that there is a set of four questions he often uses to consider the meaning of the reports he received. "The first is simply *What?* meaning essentially what is the data response to any given query. The second is *So what?* that examines whether and how the data response means anything and what some implications might be. The various responses to *So what?* suggest what further thoughts or actions might occur based on the analysis. I think this is where we might find the first occurrences of obscuring."

"You mean because determining what to think and how to act based on the raw data can be interpreted so many ways?" asked Peter.

"That's right. Even if every person has identical access to the raw data, what they do with the analysis, their *So what?* can be intentionally or unintentionally manipulated because of their own experiences, their beliefs, their biases. Essentially, the raw data is analogous to the scientific name and the various answers to *So what?* are analogous to all the subsequent common names we were talking about the other day."

"Interesting analogy," said Peter. "I think I'm following you. Please go on. You said there were four *What?* questions."

"Right. As the responses to *So what?* are considered or acted on, the next question is *Now what?* The responses to that can be fairly immediate after *So what?* or take many years to even ask the question. I think the longer it takes to ask *Now what?* the more ingrained the response to *So what?* becomes in our thinking and behaviors. We accept the *So what?* behaviors and thoughts almost unconsciously as we tell ourselves stories and give examples of why they are true without further examination, especially if they've been reinforced by culture and institutions."

Andrew asked, "Can you give an example?"

Josh said, "There are so many, and I haven't examined them in great depth. I don't know whether this will make sense. Using the idea of a possibly simple truth – Children should be protected from exploitation and allowed to grow, learn and play. That's the *What?* The *So what?* gets obscured when there are different ways people interpret that truth to have it serve their purposes. For example, in many places there was a need for children to help with the production of crops or the husbandry of taking care of livestock that produced food. For many, this was just common sense and the way things work. It was not questioned. It reinforced the values of that society and engaged children in doing work that helped with survival. In many cases, it was mainly harmless."

"However, over time, as more and more production moved off the land and we had the beginnings of the industrial revolution, often children were forced to work in the production of goods for a growing population. There were either not enough adult workers or the labor of children was paid at a much lower scale, thus serving the industrialists to make larger profits. This is an example, perhaps, of a simple truth being obscured because of how people in power wanted to leverage children in the workplace for their own purposes. They treated children as "small adults" rather than as individuals needing care and education."

Andrew interjected, "And that's the way it was in the U.S. for many years. There were plenty of people protesting that kind of exploitation. They exposed the exploitation of children and the injustices of forcing them to do manual labor. Then reform movements and new laws changed the system to protect children from those situations."

"Yes," replied Josh. "That could be the transition to the third *What?* question. Once a set of beliefs and behaviors has been in place for a while, people will sometimes ask *Now what?* Sometimes that question never arises, and things just continue as they had been and are accepted as normal. The answer to *Now what?* is generally 'more of the same.' If the situation is mainly harmless, it might be OK to just let it be. But if the beliefs and behaviors are harmful through being obscured, we need to peel back the coverings to see the truth underneath." He continued. "A friend of mine recently told me a word that I think captures this. 'Pentimento' meaning that during our process of creating something, we cover up the original to make the image what we want to be seen, even when it may hide a deeper truth."

Peter jumped in. "So the first three *What?* questions are *What?*, *So what?* and *Now what?* What's the fourth?"

Josh said, "The fourth is rarely asked while in the throes of the first three. That question is *Then what?* Like in a chess game played by a master where one thinks several moves ahead, this requires a lot of high-level strategic thinking. Playing out in one's mind various scenarios of what might happen as people adopt beliefs and behaviors based on the first two or three *What?* questions." Josh paused to think, then said, "If we continue with the truth about children – and I'm no expert in this field – it may lead us to consider how we can support and enhance the care and guidance of children to ensure they are learning and growing up to be ethical and caring adults."

Peter responded. "I like this structure of the four *What?* questions. It seems like they can help you – and us – on your mission to spread the message – Don't obscure simple truth."

Andrew added, "And also understand that some things are mainly harmless."

"Yes. I hadn't considered that methodology until we were talking today," said Josh. "I appreciate your participation. Thank you both."

Peter replied, "I'm going to do another podcast about the mission and the four *What?* questions. But Andrew...." And he gestured to his brother.

Andrew said, "I'm not just Peter's brother and supporter of his podcast. I have a radio talk show I do every Sunday morning called

Can We Talk About It? where I interview guests about what they are thinking. I'd like to have you come on the program and talk with me and my listeners about what you're doing. If you will, at least the What? and So what? parts. Would you like to do that?"

Josh was astounded. "I'm not clear on what's involved, but it sounds like a great opportunity to spread the message."

"Terrific," Andrew said. "It will take about a week to set it up and give you a bit of training for a live broadcast. Can we meet next Monday morning and start to work on it?" Andrew handed him a business card with the name and address of the station.

Josh hesitated. He believed he was more of an introvert and would not make a good radio personality. But Andrew seemed welcoming and would help him through the process. "OK. I'll meet you there at 9 am."

For his part, Peter said, "Josh I think Andrew's broadcast will help you much more than my meager podcast. I hope to see you from time to time in the park and Garden, but for now, I'm thrilled to pass you over too Andrew."

"Peter, thank you. I appreciate you helping me get more clarity on what I'm trying to do and using your podcast to start to spread the message. I look forward to working with Andrew and keeping in touch with you."

They shook hands all around and as Josh was turning to return to work, Andrew said, "Have a nice day."

Chapter 13

Clarifying the Mission

As he started the walk back toward his office, he realized that his effort to share the message with humanity had started with Mary and Commander. Now, he thought, the mission had developed a life of its own through his conversations with Peter and Andrew and the exposure they would get on future podcasts and a radio talk show. He was eager to meet with Mary and Commander to bring them up to date and reinsure himself that he was on the right path.

Once again as he neared the Bean, he spotted Mary on a bench, her cart by her side and surrounded by pigeons feasting on the bits of bread she shared. Commander was among them and noticed Josh's approach. Commander looked at Mary and deposited a large dropping near her foot. Mary studied the message and looked up to see Josh approaching. She moved down to the end of the bench along with her cart subtly indicating that Josh should take the other end of the bench. As before, they spoke quietly without looking at each other.

"I've had a few very interesting days and want to tell you both about what's been happening. I'm hoping you'll let me know if I'm moving in the right direction, or not, and what's next." Josh noted that both Mary and Commander seemed to nod at him, encouraging him to continue.

"I've had a couple of conversations with a park employee, Peter Fisher, and now his brother Andrew. Peter has a podcast and included a story and some recording of me and my mission. In his podcast he emphasized the message 'Don't obscure simple truth' and also how many obscurities are 'mainly harmless'. I've done further research using my artificial intelligence app to clarify a few simple truths and how they've been obscured throughout history for whatever reasons. Now Andrew has invited me to join him on his radio broadcast to talk more about all this." He paused his eyes moving from Mary to Commander and back to sense their response.

Mary said, "Obviously I have no way to listen to a podcast or radio broadcast. I trust what you've told us and it sounds like things are on track. How are you feeling about all this?"

Josh replied, "I'm not sure where all this is going and what I'm supposed to do. And I feel woefully out of my depth." He told them briefly about the four 'What?' questions and where he was feeling inadequate to speak to how people or institutions should think or act any differently.

"Well," replied Mary. "That might explain the message Commander just left me and what I heard in my head." She went on. "Commander said it is not for you to have the answers to 'Now what?' and 'Then What?' Your mission is to help people understand the process whereby humans obscure the truth and then to provoke thinking that will encourage dialogue, especially where people have strong differences of beliefs and opinions about what's going on."

"Hmm," said Josh. "I don't have to have the answers, just raise the questions. Or as you say, 'provoke thinking'. That makes sense because so many of the obscured truths have led to behaviors where people just continue to believe and act as they always have, as if what they believe is not only right, but is the *only* right way to think and act. Then they try to get the people they disagree with to change their minds and behaviors. Each different side of the situation digs its heels in and fights off any challenges. Some adopt a cognitive dissonance that inhibits them even considering alternative ways of thinking and acting. Some just agree to disagree without working to come to a better mutual understanding. And some go with a kind of 'might is right' set of behaviors. Whoever is more powerful gets to set the agenda of what happens."

Mary said, "Commander also put forth a warning for you. If I understand him correctly, he suggests that as more people listen to you and become aware of the message and its implications, especially as you talk about contemporary issues, some people will embrace what you're saying and others will be angered by it. Be careful!"

"Thanks. I will. I'm glad I have you and Commander with me on this."

"Yes we're here to support you. But – and this is a big but – don't tell anyone you're talking with a pigeon and a bag lady about this. They will think you're crazy and no longer pay attention. You need to take the credit for what you're thinking and sharing." She paused and looked over to Josh. "Especially don't tell anyone about me. I am still fearful that my life is in danger from Jude and his gang. Don't tell anyone about me, please!" she implored.

"Your secret is safe with me," assured Josh. But he wondered if anyone is really looking for her.

When Josh returned to his office, he used his search engine to look for any news about Flash, Flesh, and Fantasy or about Jude McBride, or any police reports. What he found substantiated the story. The FBI had raided the store and studio shortly after Corrine had left. There were a few local cops providing security and the FBI held them at gunpoint while they started to go through the studio space. Some of the cops, figuring their careers were over, pulled out their weapons and a gun battle ensued. It was quickly over with all the cops dead or seriously wounded. No FBI agent was injured as they'd all come in for the raid wearing bulletproof vests and helmets. The FBI confiscated hundreds of hours of recordings of child pornography. The news also listed the names of the store owner and all the cops who had been involved. Listed among the dead were the store owner and Jude McBride, the cop ringleader.

Corrine Randall, AKA Mary, was safe. No one was looking for her. She could get on with her life however she chose. Josh could hardly wait to tell her the news. Perhaps now, she could work by his side out in the open.

Chapter 14

Can We Talk About It?

For the next couple days Josh was extremely busy at work with some improvements the team had made in how their AI worked. The capabilities of machine learning were incredible. By providing the natural language engine with more examples from history of political writing and speeches, their app was able to create what sounded like the wisdom of the ages dealing with some contemporary issues. This was especially impressive when Josh and his team read through potential speeches that might be delivered by a politician today speaking about topics such as climate change, gun control, racial issues, and immigration. Josh was particularly impressed by the diversity of responses when they asked the program to produce multiple speeches from different perspectives. It was clear to Josh that the simple truths they were talking about were quite obscured by the slants and biases coming from 'people' on many sides of each argument. It was so real, and yet, just a simulation. Josh found himself asking *Now what?* over and over.

The realization came to him that each person or institution simulated was 'pre-programmed' for a certain response. Knowing a bit about who was talking and their paradigms of the world, you could almost predict what they would say and how they would defend their argument. Thinking about what Commander had suggested, Josh began to understand his mission was to disrupt the probable flow of explanations and arguments and to provoke thinking before people dug in their heels. And even if the different perspectives, beliefs and behaviors had been around for a very long time, Josh would encourage people to go back to the beginnings – where did the stories begin and what simple truth were they based on, and how had that truth been obscured?

He was excited to meet a couple days later on Monday at 9 am with Andrew and learn how to work together to create a live broadcast. Unlike Peter's podcasts, whatever he said in the moment is what the listeners would hear. There was to be no rehearsal or editing. This was raw. He thought, "This is like real-time data being fed into the human consciousness and potentially being obscured by people's predispositions. It was unlikely anyone could listen with a completely open mind. But that's OK. My task is to help each listener realize they are predisposed and to pause to consider if what they believe and act on is appropriate and justified." He continued his thought. "And I have to let go of any expectations of myself that I have the right answers about *So what? Now what?* and *Then what?* Those answers will develop as I provoke thinking and encourage dialogue."

The broadcast studio was in a different direction from the park. He wished he'd had time to find Mary and tell her the good news about Flash, Flesh, and Fantasy and that the store owner and Jude

McBride were dead. Corrine was safe and could choose to live her life whatever way she wanted without fear.

A studio assistant met Josh at the front desk and guided Josh back to a control booth where Andrew was waiting for him. "Good morning, Josh. It's great to see you. How are you feeling?"

"Hi Andrew. Good to see you. too. As to how I'm feeling – I have to be honest - I'm very nervous. I'm someone who generally keeps to himself and don't talk to many people. And even if I don't see anyone, I'll know they're listening and scrutinizing everything I say."

"That's honest, Josh. Perhaps it will help you to imagine it's just the two of us talking, not too dissimilar from our conversation the other day in the garden. And, the live part will be 15 minutes and airs at 7 in the morning on a Sunday so there won't be a huge audience. Just relax. Be yourself. I'll say a few things and ask you questions just like a normal conversation." Andrew paused and studied his guest. "Josh, I think you have something to share that is important for my listeners to hear. Remember that."

For the next hour Andrew showed Josh how the equipment works and a few more things. They put on headsets and spoke through mics doing sound checks. They'd do this more before they went live, but it would not be so tense given that they'd practiced. They also talked through a few comments and questions they'd each make as the program progressed. It wasn't a script so much as bullet point prompts if things needed to move along or change direction. By the time they finished and Josh headed to work, he felt more confident that he could handle this.

As he headed back toward his office his thoughts were racing. Intertwining of self-doubt and a sense of purpose had him going in circles. He consciously worked to slow his breathing and to calm himself. "You were chosen," he said to himself. "You're on a mission that is much more significant than anything you've ever done. All the signs are showing you this path. Trust the journey." The self-talk worked a bit, and by the time he reached his cubicle, he was able again to focus on his work assignments.

As the day wore on, he was aware that his mind kept wandering to questions about the mission. The challenge to talk live on the radio, despite Andrew's assurances, was becoming a distraction. "Or," he wondered, "is it my job that is the distraction?"

He found his co-worker, John, in the breakroom and decided to tell him about some of what was going on. He shared about his mission to spread the message – 'Don't obscure simple truth' – being careful to leave out anything about Mary and Commander. He told John about his first kind-of-scary excursion into Lurie Garden and how his fears dissipated as he met and talked with Peter Fischer. He told John that Peter had made a recording and produced a podcast aired as Experiences in the Garden.

"Then I went back a few days later for more conversation and he introduced me to his brother, Andrew. The three of us talked through a couple more examples of simple truths that had been obscured through history and why it might be important to provoke thinking about them." Josh paused. "Then Andrew said he produced a weekly radio talk program every Sunday at 7 am and that he'd like me to come on the air and share some of what I was thinking about. He thought his listeners would be interested."

"Wow, Josh!" responded John. "That doesn't sound like the Josh I've known. I've always recognized that you thought a bit differently than many of us about the work we do. We all saw the same data, but you always seemed to ask the next question, like

'What does it all mean?' I can see you talking on the radio to raise all kinds of questions."

"Thanks, John. I appreciate the support and encouragement. I hope I can do this."

"You can do it!" supported John. I can't wait to listen to the podcasts and the radio program. Good luck."

They both went back to work on their projects. Josh felt more confident after hearing John's encouragement. For his part, John was curious to listen to the podcasts and radio program to better understand what Josh was thinking.

As the days passed, Josh periodically used some time and computing power to further explore examples of simple truths and various ways they were obscured and how those obfuscations led to different kinds of behaviors. He wanted to do his homework so he'd have something to talk about with Andrew.

And John made time after work to listen to the two podcasts that Peter had made. He was intrigued by some of what he heard. At work and with a few friends, he shared about what he'd heard and encouraged them to listen to the podcasts and possibly tune in next Sunday morning to hear Josh on the radio. He didn't tell Josh that he'd spread the word concerned that it might make Josh uncomfortable.

The next Sunday morning, after a fitful night sleep and two cups of strong coffee, Josh arrived at the radio station at 5:30 am. He had a few pages of notes he'd made that he believed would help him if he got flummoxed.

"Good morning, Josh," greeted Andrew and his assistant. "Good to see you. Would you like a cup of coffee or anything?"

"No, thank you. I've already had two cups and my mind is racing. Perhaps just some water."

Andrew and Josh moved into the recording studio and settled in. They put on headsets, did mic checks and talked through a few ideas about how the conversation would go. At 7, they were on the air. After a few minutes Josh got over most of his jitters and had a comfortable conversation with Andrew. It was just as Andrew had suggested. It felt like just the two of them talking pleasantly and no distracting thoughts of who might be listening and what they might be thinking.

Andrew had started out describing how his brother Peter had met Josh at Lurie Garden in Millenium Park, then about Peter's podcasts relating that Josh was on a mission to spread the message 'Don't obscure simple truth'. Andrew also shared how Josh and Peter decided that many truths were obscured over time, but in many of those cases, the responses to those obscurities were mainly harmless. However, there were numerous cases where the interpretations of some truths led to different responses from which conflict often arose.

"Yes," said Josh. "That's where we need to pause our thinking and examine our personal experiences and beliefs. At times, we seem to just follow whatever we've always been taught without being open to the possibility that there are other ways to look at the simple truth." Josh gave a few brief examples from various spheres of the human experience based on the research he'd done and the notes he'd made. "Consider the discovery of what causes disease. The simple truth is that microscopic organisms cause many diseases. But before Flemming's accidental discovery of penicillin, the invention of the microscope and the germ theory we mostly accept today, some people believed diseases were caused by bad behaviors, by demons, as some form of punishment and so on. Responses varied from wearing long robes and waving wands to prevent or cure disease - many of those were mainly harmless - to suggesting that some people were witches and had cursed the individual. Some of those beliefs led to persecution or even death for people believed to be practitioners. Research by Louis Pasteur, Robert Koch and others led to discoveries and treatments. And today, we continue to develop medicines and vaccines to prevent or treat many maladies affecting our bodies."

As the session was approaching the planned end time, Andrew asked Josh "So, how do you see your role in spreading this message?"

After a bit of a pause, Josh said, "I don't have the answers to all that we humans should do. I think I'm here to provoke thinking; to encourage people to examine their own beliefs and behaviors and how consciously or unconsciously we each may obscure simple truth. Like Socrates and the Scottish philosopher, David Hume, I consider myself a gadfly, someone who persistently challenges the status quo, people in power, or popular positions." He paused. "Actually," thought Josh out loud, "It goes beyond just challenging people's ideas. It also involves consideration of the impact on others and the planet. I intend more than to just provoke thinking. I intend to provoke thoughtfulness and to do it with kindness and no judgment."

"Well," Andrew said. "Provoking thoughtfulness could be a way of encouraging people to rethink their positions about what is true.

I could see that it might also rile some others to more fiercely defend their positions."

Andrew said, "Josh, as we close this segment of our broadcast, what would you suggest others might do to carry this forward?"

Josh didn't hesitate. "Anyone interested might do online searches, talk with others, or just think to themselves – 'What are some simple truths and how have they been obscured through history?' Then consider, 'And what difference does it make?' Anyone and everyone can provoke thoughtfulness and come away with more clarity of why they think, believe and act as they do and the impact of various ideas."

Then Andrew surprised Josh by saying, "I think our listeners would like to hear more from you about all this. Can we expect you back again next week?"

"Uh, OK. If you think it would be useful."

"Absolutely! Thanks for listening this morning, everyone. We've given you a few things to think about and we'll talk more next Sunday. And, Josh Carpenter, thanks for being with us today and provoking thoughtfulness."

They signed off and Andrew shook Josh's hand enthusiastically. "That was great, Josh. I think you've stimulated some interesting thinking. I look forward to talking with you again next week."

Chapter 15

Spreading the Message

Josh kept very busy with work and now his preparations for weekly broadcasts. He got into the park every few days but never saw Mary or Commander. He missed them and was eager to share his experiences. Afterall, he was spreading the message as he'd been asked to do. Their absence, although a bit disconcerting, was not immobilizing. He felt his sense of purpose and was acting to pass the message.

Over the next several weeks, every Sunday morning Josh was on the radio with Andrew sharing more examples of simple truths, how they may have been obscured, and the implications for individuals, institutions and society. The program appeared to be getting noticed by more and more people.

In one particular broadcast, Josh shared his thoughts about things people say by rote, perhaps without thinking, but mainly harmless. One example he used was how often people say things like 'Have a nice day' or 'God bless you' when someone sneezes. People are just being polite. 'Have a nice day' is mainly harmless, but 'God bless you' has more in the statement than just being polite. There are implications about who or what is god, whether someone believes in that entity, or the implications that such an entity is even aware of an individual's sneeze and is watching over them.

After closing the broadcast one week, Andrew told Josh that the studio wanted to change up the format a bit. First, they wanted to make it a two-hour program broadcast live on Sunday morning with a recorded episode on a weekday morning. They still wanted Josh to be the initiator to provoke thoughtfulness, and they wanted to bring in experts – historians, scientists, theologians – to further discuss the development of various interpretations of some of the simple truths.

For his part, in his mind and often shared in the broadcasts, Josh reminded people that he was not an expert. He was simply asking questions and encouraging people to examine their own beliefs and behaviors. Most of the programs included that disclaimer and then an examination of what Josh suggested was a simple truth. The experts fleshed out the various interpretations of those truths and gave examples of the impact those interpretations have had throughout history and to the present day.

Some of the topics were pretty straightforward and mainly harmless. But others were rather controversial and led to strong debates about the merits and implications of the truth. Some of the most strongly debated were about

- Civil Rights: all people regardless of race, ethnicity, religious affiliation, gender or gender identity deserve equal rights and treatment

- War: war causes immense human suffering and rarely yields clear victories that last

- Environment: the health of the planet is essential for human survival

The discussions, actually debates, were often rigorous and exhausting. Josh kept his role clear. He was to remind people – 'Don't obscure simple truth', many obscurities are 'mainly harmless', and to 'provoke thoughtfulness'. He stayed away from suggesting any particular outcomes were better or worse than others. "That's for each person or institution to discuss through thoughtful self-examination and discourse."

Josh had not paid much attention beyond being in the broadcasts and keeping an eye out for Mary or Commander. So, at work when John asked, "Josh, have you seen the newspaper article about your broadcasts?" Josh responded that he wasn't aware that anyone was listening.

John said, "Well I've been listening and telling others to do so. The word has spread and there was an article in the Tribune talking about the phenomenon. Basically, many people are having open conversations about how they developed their thinking and belief systems. They are questioning where and how they got their ideas and if they are accurate."

"That's good, I guess" replied Josh. "I mean, that's kind of what I hoped would happen."

"And," John enthused, "there is a big marketing push. People are buying stickers for their cars that say, 'Don't obscure simple truth' and there are hats and T-shirts that say 'Mainly harmless' or 'Provoke thoughtfulness'."

Josh wasn't sure how he felt about what John was telling him. It felt like the message was getting commercialized and some people were trying to make a profit off it. Perhaps they were obscuring the simple truth by their actions.

As he neared his office, he decided to take a brief detour to see if he could find Mary to share the news about her past employment and relieve her fear of being found. As expected, he spotted her sitting on a park bench, her pushcart next to her. She was not feeding the birds like usual. He did not see Commander. Or for that matter, Princess, Goldie, or Peace. "Strange," he thought. "They always seem to know where she is and gather around."

As he neared the bench, he could hear that she was not mumbling. She was crying softly. He rushed over and knelt in front of her. "Mary, what's going on? Why are you crying? Where are the pigeons?"

"Oh Josh," she cried. "It's terrible. An hour ago I was feeding the pigeons and talking with Commander. All of a sudden, the birds were all covered by netting. Then some people from animal control approached, and rolling the net back little by little, they captured each bird and put them in cages. Then they loaded the cages on a truck." She sobbed loudly. "I asked them, 'What's going on? What are you doing? Where are you taking them? What will happen to them?' The worker said 'Thank you for helping us capture them. We've been watching you feed them and set up our net traps in places you often sit. We could not have caught so many without your help.'" She sobbed even more. "It's my fault they were captured. Who knows what will happen to them? Oh, poor Commander. And Princess, Goldie and Peace, too. What have I done?" she moaned.

Josh realized this was not the time to tell her about the demise of Flash, Flesh and Fantasy and Jude. She needed comfort and support with this crisis. "I'm so sorry that this happened," he said, and tried to comfort her without much success. After several minutes, he stood up and said, "I'll try to find out where they've taken them. I'll do what I can."

Josh looked around and spotted the animal control crew about fifty yards away at another capture site. He jogged over and got a worker's attention. "What's going on?" he asked.

"We're reducing the pigeon population in the park. Lately it's been growing quickly for some reason and their droppings are everywhere. The public is complaining, and we were directed to help Streets and Sanitation remove as many pigeons as we can."

"Well, what do you do with them?"

"As with any animal situation like this, the birds will be processed at the Flint Creek Wildlife Rehabilitation Facility in Barrington. Healthy birds will be released through the forest preserves around northern Illinois. Any sick or injured bird will be treated and released as appropriate. Any bird they consider unable to survive will be euthanized."

"Sounds like a big job. How long does it take before healthy birds are released?" asked Josh.

"Up to a couple days depending on how many there are and where they're taken to be released."

Josh thanked the worker and made his way back to where he'd left Mary. She was still on the same bench, whimpering softly, but a bit calmer. Josh filled her in on what he'd learned and after a few more minutes trying to comfort and reassure her, he left promising to check back the next day.

Chapter 16

The Shelter

The next morning, even before he went to the office, Josh walked around the park looking for Mary. He didn't see her in any of the usual places and was concerned that something might have happened to her – even that she might have blamed herself for the pigeons being captured and done something drastic.

"Work will just have to wait," he said to himself. "Mary needs me."

As he continued to make his way around the park, on his third loop he spotted a patrol officer. He didn't want to get Mary into any trouble but figured this might be the fastest way to find out what happened to her.

"Excuse me officer," he said as he approached the man. "I'm looking for a woman – you might say a bag lady – who frequents this park. I have something I want to give her, but I can't find her today."

"Oh, you probably mean Mary. Yeah, we see her all the time around here. She keeps mostly to herself, not bothering anyone, so we leave her alone. Last evening, one of our guys found her crying and mumbling that something was all her fault. He tried talking with her, but she wouldn't calm down. They were concerned she might hurt herself or upset people, so they took her to the Pacific Garden Mission on South Canal Street. They turned her over to an on-site counselor and left."

"Thank you, officer. I think I'll go check on her."

Josh used a rideshare app and got dropped off at the shelter. Upon entering, he went up to the receptionist and announced who he was and that he was a friend of Mary and wanted to check on her. Naturally, the receptionist had been trained to be suspicious of anyone, especially a male, coming to the Mission claiming to be a friend of a woman sheltering there. After some back and forth where Josh convinced the receptionist and a supervisor that he'd been told by the police that they'd brought Mary there last evening and that she was extremely agitated, they neither affirmed nor denied that she was there, but asked Josh to wait while they did some checking.

Several minutes later, the supervisor motioned for Josh to follow her to a private room where they could talk. "Josh, Mary is here. She's doing much better this morning after getting a shower, some food, and a good night's sleep. She wouldn't tell us her full name nor anything about her circumstances. She also declined our invitation to join us in our prayer service this morning. But when I told her someone was here to check on her and gave her your name, she brightened up a bit. She said she'd like to see you."

Josh let out a sigh of relief. "Thank you for all you've already done for her. That's very kind."

The supervisor directed Josh to wait in the room while she went to get Mary. She also informed Josh that she would stay in the room while they talked to ensure Mary's safety and comfort.

A few minutes later, Mary was ushered into the room. As soon as she saw Josh she ran over to him and hugged him. Then, she quickly backed off realizing they did not have that kind of relationship. She smiled at him and said, "Thank you for coming to see me Josh. I'm doing much better now, especially since you're here." And turning toward the supervisor, said, "I'd like to leave with him now and go back where I came from."

The supervisor initially said that couldn't happen. That there were protocols and paperwork that needed to be completed. They went back and forth with Mary refusing to provide anything further about who she was or her circumstances. Josh, although having no legal status in the situation, stood by her as she made her arguments.

"This is a free country. You cannot hold me here against my will. I've done nothing wrong!" Mary shouted. "I want out!"

The supervisor tried calmly to convince Mary that this was a safe place. That they would look after her welfare physically, emotionally and spiritually. Mary was adamant and getting more and more agitated. Finally, the supervisor acknowledged that they had no legal, only moral, grounds to retain her. With no formal paperwork identification or signatures, they let Mary go with encouragement to Josh to take care of her.

They collected Mary's belongings and her pushcart and got a rideshare back to Millennium Park. Josh walked with Mary to a bench she'd chosen. He explained what he'd learned about the great pigeon roundup and that he would see if he could learn more. She was much calmer and asked to just be left alone. Reluctantly, Josh agreed and went to his office.

Later in the day, realizing he hadn't told Mary about Flash, Flesh, and Fantasy and that Jude was no more, he took another walk to the park. He found Mary right where he'd left her a few hours before. She was much calmer and seemed resigned to her situation, for now. Some kind person had given her a sandwich and bottle of water. And as typical for Mary, she saved the bread for the birds, whichever might approach.

Josh sat at the far end of the bench with Mary's pushcart between them. He looked at her until she sensed his stare and looked back at him. "Mary, this is important and has nothing to do with the pigeons or the message. This is about you." He paused to be sure she was tracking. "I did a bit of research and found out that shortly after you left Boston, the FBI raided and shut down your old employer. There was a gun fight and the store owner, Jude McBride and a few other cops were killed." He paused again. "Mary, it's over. You can now go back to being Corrine Randall and restart your life as you want it to be."

Mary inhaled deeply then let it all out. She started to cry, this time from relief rather than sorrow. "I can have my life back!?" she exclaimed. "Oh my. I don't know what to say."

Josh reached out and laid his hand on her arm clothed in the torn coat she'd been wearing for a few months. "Just take it all in, Corrine. Let it wash over you and we'll talk more tomorrow about how you want to move forward." He paused. "And, when you're ready, I have a lot to tell you about how I'm doing spreading the message."

Mary was so taken with the news she pretty much missed the part about the message. "OK. You know where to find me tomorrow and we'll talk."

Chapter 17

Commercialization

Late the next morning Josh stopped at the deli and got some pastry, two sandwiches, two cups of coffee, two bottles of water and two apples. He was excited to see Mary and, perhaps, more openly share some food and time together. He knew she'd still be mourning the loss of Commander but was hopeful the news he'd shared about her past no longer chasing her, would elicit more a sense of freedom for her.

As he walked through the park, he spotted her on one of her normal benches. Even from a distance, he could see that there was something different going on. As he got closer, he noticed that she was once again surrounded by pigeons and was tossing out pieces of bread. He could hear her mumbling as she spoke with the birds just as she'd been doing the first time he met her several weeks ago.

And to his great surprise, Commander was right there, front and center. "Is that Commander?" whispered Josh as he sat down on the bench. "And Princess, and Goldie and Peace, too?"

Mary turned to him with a big smile and tears of joy on her face. "Yes. They're back. If I understand correctly, they were released in a place far from here. Commander somehow had the capabilities usually found only in homing pigeons, and he found his way back here. Princess, Goldie and Peace flew with him and, almost like a squadron, they landed at my feet about an hour ago. They all danced around and left many messages."

"That's amazing," uttered Josh. "What a relief to know they're ok."

He pulled out the food and drinks he had brought. "Now that you don't need to be afraid of being found anymore, I thought we'd celebrate with some pastries and coffee, or perhaps an early lunch. I think we can talk more openly and not wonder if it's safe to be seen together," he suggested.

"Yes, I think that's right," she replied. "Josh, I appreciate so much all you've done for me and especially following Commander's wish that you spread the message." She paused. "I know I can go back to being Corrine Randall, but I don't believe that's my destiny. I have become Mary and will continue to help Commander recruit disciples to spread the message."

Again she paused. "You may have suspected you weren't the first. Before I met you, I spoke with a few of the homeless people in the park as selected by Commander. I explained to them what I told you and a few seemed to get it. They walked through the park, stayed at shelters, rode the 'L' and tried to tell people about how humans have obscured truth through the ages. Most were not successful in spreading that message but at least had some success in encouraging kindness and generosity. I also understand from Commander's messages that there have been others like me who have been communicated with and who have tried to pass on the message. But it's been with only a little success. It wasn't until the unique combination of me as Mary and you, Josh Carpenter, with your unique life circumstances and the way you've trained your brain to analyze large amounts of data, that things have come together, and the message is being spread effectively."

Josh was looking at her incredulously. "You mean this," and he gestured at the pigeons, "has been going on for a while?"

"Yes," and not just with pigeons. Many animals, wild and domesticated, have been trying to communicate with people for a long time. Evidently, there has been very little progress up to this point. Most of the messengers have been ignored, some even locked away in institutions and marked as having mental problems. Some even disappeared. This is not an easy mission you are on."

She continued. "Even though I understand that I am free to resume my life as Corrine Randall and follow whatever path I choose, the future of humanity demands that I keep on as Mary and help you for as long as I can."

For his part, Josh just listened and sat with his mouth agape, his eyes darting back and forth between Mary and the pigeons. "I don't know what to say," uttered Josh. "I guess I'm not surprised that there have been others. I think I may have even encountered some of them without realizing who they were. And yes, I think that I have been fortunate to meet Peter Fischer who put me on his podcast. Then to meet his brother, Andrew, who for several weeks has been talking with me and a few experts on the radio. And my co-worker, John, tells me that there was an article in the Tribune."

Just then, a small group of young people walked along the path in front of them. Most were dressed in jeans and T-shirts or hoodies, some wearing ball caps. Three different ones were emblazoned with sayings on their outerwear.

Josh couldn't help himself. He jogged over to the front of the group and calmly held up his hands to show he wanted to talk. Josh pointed to their clothing and asked, "What's with all these sayings?"

A short woman waved her hands at her fellows and said "Have you been in a cave, man? This dude is talking on the radio about how people have been deceiving themselves or others for a long time and that it's time we paid attention to where our thoughts, beliefs and actions come from." She pointed to her own T-shirt. "Don't obscure simple truth," she said. "That's the whole, simple message. What James is wearing," she said gesturing to a guy in the group, "says we should 'provoke thoughtfulness'. We take that to mean raise questions of ourselves and others to encourage considering where our ideas come from and also to do it in a kind and open way. And Phillip's cap says 'Mainly harmless' which reminds us not to take things too seriously. Lots of the ways people have interpreted things have not led to significant problems. This dude is speaking our language!"

Josh nodded. "Thanks for letting me know. I guess I have been in a cave of sorts recently. I had no idea that so much was going on."

One of the group said, "If you want to get in on it, there are a few vendors selling stuff with these sayings on them. You can get stuff like we're wearing, or mugs, banners, bumper stickers. You name it. They're everywhere." As they moved along, one of the group turned and said, "Have a nice day, man."

Josh felt a bit lightheaded as he walked back over and sat down next to Mary on the bench. "I guess I haven't been paying as much attention as perhaps I should," Josh stated. "It seems like the message is being spread. It's almost like a fad, though. I'm not sure that was the intention."

Mary put her hand on Josh's arm and said, "Commander thinks it's ok that this is happening. But he also said it's time to raise some more difficult questions."

"Like what?" Josh asked.

"Questions about some of the more contemporary issues that society is facing. Some where the simple truths are more obscured than others. Ones that are not mainly harmless, but that are causing much friction and fighting among people today."

"Yes, I think Andrew and I were heading that way already. What makes you think this is the time?"

"When the police took me to the shelter, I received compassionate care and counseling. They let me take a shower and gave me food and a place to sleep for the night. It was very kind. But then, in the morning, I started to feel pressured to partake in their religious experiences. I was told that the Gospel of Jesus Christ is preached faithfully four times daily before meals and before bedtime. Further they explained that all services follow a traditional format and an invitation to receive Jesus Christ as Savior and Lord." She paused. "Well, that might work for some, but that's not for me. I know some of the homeless people who have gone to various shelters have also felt pressured. Even some of the people I had passed along Commander's message to told me they no longer felt they could spread that word because they'd been told to spread a different message."

Josh picked up on her reactions. "I think for most people who practice some religion, they don't consider themselves brainwashed. And for many, it provides a sense of comfort and security believing that some entity or institution is watching over and caring for them. Some institutions and their followers do good work in their communities. I think much of religion is mainly harmless."

"But Josh, even if it's mainly harmless for those who believe, by choice or indoctrination, I don't go in for all that God and Jesus stuff. I don't believe in any of that. Josh, you saved me from that."

She continued with strong emphasis. "I think you have to raise some questions about beliefs in some all-powerful, all-knowing non- human entity that is given credit for everything from creating the universe, giving dominion to humans over all things on the planet, and is considered by some to be watching over them personally and protecting them from harm, even promising upon death, that there's someplace they'll go to live happily ever after. It sounds like a fairy tale."

"Wow, I can tell you feel strongly about this. How come?" asked Josh.

"There are so many reasons, Josh. If there is such an entity, why would it allow suffering and evil? In just my own experience, why would such an entity allow children to be exploited and used to make pornographic films? And beyond my own experience, why do good people suffer from poverty, homelessness, disease and so on while some others get to accumulate wealth and power at the expense of the less privileged? What are the simple truths that have been obscured by people and institutions that practice those religious beliefs?"

"You've certainly got me thinking. These are questions I will think about and bring up in the next broadcast." Josh paused. "But for now, Mary, I am seeing a different aspect of you. You are not just the intermediary to Commander. You're passionate and articulate about this. Now that you're no longer threatened by exposure, I'd like you to take a seat at the table to talk about these things yourself."

"No, Josh. It's true that I no longer have to fear Jude and his gang. But you have already started to be noticed as the torch bearer. And, as a male, I think people will listen to you more than me. And, I have decided to remain as the Mary. I've chosen to work in my own special way to spread the message. I think you need to keep me out of this or risk diminishing your impact."

As she finished her speech, Commander flitted over and deposited a large dropping next to Josh's foot. Josh reacted. "I guess he agrees with you."

After several more minutes of conversation and sharing some food, Josh said his goodbyes and went back to his office. His mind was ablaze with the possibilities of raising the bar in his conversations with Andrew.

Chapter 18

Politics

When Josh called Andrew at the radio station he enthusiastically said, "I've got two topics I want to bring up in the next few broadcasts. I think they are very important for deepening the conversation although perhaps a bit riskier because of what beliefs and behaviors may be questioned."

"That sounds intriguing," responded Andrew. "What are those topics?"

"Politics and religion," said Josh. "They are potentially much more controversial and you may get some push back from your sponsors."

Andrew laughed. "Our sponsors couldn't be happier. The reports show the increase in listeners has nearly tripled their profits because of the number of people tuning in." He paused. "But now, the powers that be of this media empire are saying that people are calling and writing in that more than the voice, they want to see the person who's been causing this stir. We'll do our next few broadcasts on politics. As usual, I'll line up a few experts to share their views. We'll do the live radio broadcasts and share recordings that people can stream as they wish later in the week."

He continued. "Then, Josh, you've been invited to do a segment on The Week Ahead television program two weeks from this Sunday morning. They'll work with you at the Chicago affiliate. I understand you'll be interviewed by a new local host, Thomas Bartholome. You'll need to get there about 5:30 am to go through the preparations. Peter and I have been invited to sit in the TV audience so we can support you in that way. Is there anyone else you'd like to invite to be in the audience for support?"

Josh thought immediately of Mary but rejected that idea based on their last conversation. She wanted to remain in the background. She had said that her destiny was to help Josh understand Commander's thoughts and work through his talking points. Further she felt she had to find other messengers as pointed out by Commander. Josh said, "I do have a friend at work, John Baptiste, who might enjoy the experience. I'll ask him."

They left it there and confirmed when Josh would arrive at the studio to prepare for the next radio program. At that time, he'd meet the invited experts and they'd talk about politics.

Andrew opened the program. "My dear listeners, today Josh Carpenter and I are going to continue our conversations about the message he's been spreading – 'Don't obscure simple truth'. He warned me that this next topic may stir up some strong reactions because it's about politics. Please note – politics have been a part of human culture since time immemorial and wherever humans have been found. Today's conversation will focus primarily on current-day politics and mostly in the United States, as that's where most of our listeners are. However, much of what will be shared could apply to many other places and times."

Andrew continued his introductory remarks. "We have with us in the studio Jason Slater, a spokesperson for the Democratic party in Chicago, Martha Ramsey, a spokesperson for the Republican party for the state of Illinois, and Keith Solderheim, a candidate running as a Libertarian to be a Senator for the state of Illinois. So, get ready to experience some provoking thoughtfulness. Josh, why don't you kick it off?"

Josh began. "As Andrew suggested, the topic of politics can bring up some strong beliefs and emotions for some people. I remind you that I am not here to provide answers, but to encourage each of us, our representatives and candidates, and our institutions, to examine where our ideas and beliefs come from and how they affect our actions."

He continued. "So as we look down through history, we see countless examples of how governments and people in power have selected what they consider to be the truth and have influenced their followers to act in certain ways to reinforce their beliefs. The simple truth might be 'Governments exist to establish order, provide security, protect individual rights, and promote the general welfare of their people." He looked at the guests who were each nodding in agreement.

"Our three guests have all nodded that they agree with this simple truth. I'm guessing that each person has some different interpretations of that simple truth as we can all see by the way the political parties talk and act based on their understandings and desires."

Andrew jumped in to facilitate the conversation. "Let's give each of you a few moments to tell us where your political focus is. Perhaps indicate your party's top two areas of importance. After that we'll dig in deeper. Jason, let's start with you. How do you and members of the Democratic Party describe the role of government?"

Jason opened with, "Thank you Andrew and Josh for inviting us to this conversation. I think Democrats in general would say all the functions mentioned by Josh are important. When it comes to what we believe should be the main role of government it's to protect the rights and liberties of the people. Individual freedoms and rights such as free speech, equality, and due process must be upheld and protected from infringement. The second most important role of government is providing public goods and services. The government has to manage essential services like education, healthcare, infrastructure, and public safety that can't be managed as effectively by the private sector."

"Thank you, Jason. Martha, would you go next and tell us the two most important areas that Republicans focus on?"

"Certainly," Martha replied. "And thanks for having us today to discuss this. For Republicans, we also think all these areas are important. We tend to give more focus to maintaining order and security. The government has to establish and enforce laws to maintain the social order and protect our citizens from internal or external threats. That includes policing, the judiciary, and national defense. I suggest our second focus is on promoting economic stability and growth. The government must regulate the marketplace, control inflation, set and collect taxes, and maintain a stable and functioning economy."

"Thank you, Martha. And Keith, what are the top two areas Libertarians focus on?"

"I also want to thank Andrew and Josh for having us here today," replied Keith. "I'm sure this will be very interesting. Libertarians prioritize personal responsibility and voluntary cooperation over government control in both social and economic matters. We want to ensure maximum personal freedom in all aspects of life, including free speech, personal choices, property rights, and economic freedom. We believe that individuals should have the right to live as they choose, as long as they do not harm others. This extends to issues like drug legalization, gun rights, free markets, and privacy rights. We believe government should be as small as possible, intervening only to protect individual rights, enforce contracts, and ensure national defense. We oppose excessive regulations, high taxes, and government programs that interfere with free markets or personal choices. Our focus is on reducing government spending, eliminating unnecessary bureaucracy, and decentralizing power."

Andrew motioned to Josh to jump in. "Thank you each for your succinct responses. I remind you and our listeners that we are not here to determine who has the best response to the role of government, but to try to understand where their ideas originated, how they've evolved, and what behaviors emanate based on the thinking and beliefs underlying each political philosophy." Josh continued. "For as far back as at least Socrates and Plato in ancient Greece, there have been debates on what form of government would be best. I don't believe anyone came up with a universally accepted answer and in this present day, as each of you explained, there are various ways that we here in the United States apply our thinking.

So, I ask each of you now to help us understand how your party, or you personally, arrived at your current way of thinking."

A lively conversation ensued with much back and forth, mostly congenial. Occasionally Andrew would redirect the conversation or indicate to Josh to see if he had another question. Over the two hours, it seemed clear, at least to Josh, that each person had come to their current position because of how they were raised, taught, and influenced by important people in their lives. Each had also done some personal self-examination, reading and talking with others that either challenged or validated their thinking. And, to Josh, it seemed that each had come to their beliefs over time and had consciously or unconsciously reinforced them which further highlighted their different philosophies.

As the end of the program neared, Josh acknowledged, "The three of you, despite your different perspectives, seemed willing to listen to each other even if you strongly disagreed. I take that as a hopeful sign for our country. However, as we all know, the spectrum of viewpoints is quite wide, and we can identify several issues on which people seem to be quite polarized and unwilling to consider viewpoints that are very different from their own. Why do you think that might be the case and what do you recommend we do to address this concern?"

Andrew handled the responses. They all pretty much agreed that this particular discussion was constructive and genteel, partly because it was facilitated and partly because they knew if they dug in their heels anywhere, that Josh would question where their strong feelings and beliefs came from. They acknowledged that they learned and practiced most of their beliefs because that's what they were taught at an early age. They added that how they lived their lives, who they typically spoke with or who they avoided, consistently reinforced and deepened their thinking and belief that they were right, or at least better than the others. They further acknowledged that some people in politics or other positions of power often employed strategies and behaviors intended to minimize or belittle the thoughts and actions of people with whom they disagreed. There were even examples of prominent people reduced to name-calling and schoolyard bullying tactics to rile their adversaries or energize their base. Little effort seemed to be made to listen for commonalities or to explore whether there might be any merit in someone else's perspective. Some went as far as using media, especially social media, to further their own agendas or to block others from doing so if they disagreed or questioned.

The recommendation was to have further open conversations where anyone and everyone had a chance to be heard and listened to with respect. Unfortunately, they all also agreed that given the current environment, it was highly unlikely to happen.

"One final comment and an invitation to our listeners," said Andrew. "When Josh asked questions about where some of the political ideologies originated and how they diverged over time, our guests all suggested one possibility was the influence various religious philosophies and practices have had on politics.

Although in the U.S. we talk about the separation of church and state, the distinctions are not always clear. We'll talk more about this with Josh and a couple of guests in two weeks as we focus on how simple truths might have been obscured by various religions."

He paused. "Many of you have been writing or calling in wanting to see Josh and learn more about him. So our parent company has arranged for Josh to appear on The Week Ahead next Sunday morning. So please tune into that show next Sunday morning then join us again in two weeks here on Can We Talk About It? …"

Chapter 19

Self-Doubt

When Josh left the studio following the broadcast, he was experiencing a mixture of feelings. One was pride about the success of his efforts to spread the message originating from Commander as relayed to him through Mary – 'Don't obscure simple truth'. A second was that of an imposter asking himself who he thought he was being a vocal and public personality talking with people about the various topics they'd been discussing on Andrew's program. A third was a growing uneasiness about whether the ideas he was sharing were coming from Commander – a pigeon – for goodness' sakes! How did he know the extent to which these were the thoughts somehow passed along from a pigeon, or a bag lady-in-hiding, versus his own thoughts?

He decided he needed to meet with Mary and Commander to try to gain some clarity to sort through these feelings.

He found Mary sitting on a bench to the side of the Crown Fountain. The fountain consists of two 50-foot-tall structures that display the faces of Chicagoans. Mary liked to come here to watch the children, and occasionally adults, splash around in the reflecting pool and stand under the water periodically spouting from the mouths of the diverse faces. As per usual, she was surrounded by several pigeons including Commander and his followers.

"Hi Mary" he started, then with a glance toward the ground to his right, "and Commander. I've just come from doing another radio broadcast with Andrew Fischer. I'm having a bit of self-doubt about what's going on and my role in it." He went on to share some of his ambivalence.

Commander seemed to be listening closely, tilting his head from side to side or nodding up and down. He walked around in little circles and produced several droppings. Josh was a bit amused by the antics but frustrated as well. "Mary, I don't hear Commander in my thoughts. We don't have any telepathic communication. And I can't read any message in his droppings. So, I depend on you to interpret everything for me. Even though what you say makes some sense, how do I know it's accurate and coming from him, not just something you're making up or even just in my own head?"

"Commander understands," she replied. "Like many prophets and messengers throughout human history, some people have felt called upon to relay a message to humanity. They often question where they get their ideas, some suggesting they are directed by some higher power or supreme being. They also ask 'Why me' and 'Why now'. Many experience a crisis of trust and give up their pursuit. Only a few have been around and influential enough to have made some small difference. And unfortunately, most of them are not listened to, are belittled, threatened, or even imprisoned or killed to prevent any disruption to the powers that be in their times. It is a considerable undertaking."

"Yes," responded Josh. "Those are some of my questions, too. Let's start with why me?"

Mary looked at Commander for a brief moment, then said, "Commander says, 'Why not you? Anyone might be capable of delivering the message and we have worked with many through the ages, and even in the present times. Not everyone is successful in understanding the message and getting heard. You've proven to be extraordinary, perhaps because of your background and the way your mind works to understand problems and work for a solution.'"

"Thanks for the flattery although I still have questions about that." He continued, "and why now?"

Again, after looking at Commander, Mary replied, "It is not just now. It is ongoing and everywhere. But the times and conditions are ripe for getting the message out to more people now because of the many current issues people are facing here and elsewhere. Many people are concerned about civil rights, continued warfare, rights to life, rights to express themselves authentically, especially concerning gender identity, and very important to all beings on the planet, the effects of human activity on climate change and the effect it is having on all life forms."

Josh stood quietly and considered what he'd heard. Then, "And from what you said earlier, most of the people trying to pass along the message have not been listened to, have been belittled, threatened, imprisoned or killed. Am I in danger?"

With another look at Commander who also left a big dropping, Mary said, "Yes. There will likely be some supportive reactions such as you've seen with sayings on some people's apparel and bumper stickers, but there will also be those who don't like what you're saying. There will be protests, and threats, and who knows what else. But we're going to keep watch and protect you as best we can."

"Wow," responded Josh. "I didn't understand what I was getting myself into. I feel a bit manipulated."

"Would you have taken this on if you were aware of all the opportunities and challenges ahead of you? We all go through our lives with various degrees of possible rewards and risks. If we knew everything ahead of time, would we even continue?"

Josh replied a bit angrily. "It's ironic. We're talking about how we mustn't obscure simple truths, yet it sounds like the simple truth that my life might be in danger was intentionally hidden from me."

"It is what it is, Josh. Every moment you get to choose if and how you continue. The outcome is not pre-determined. But when you sense a purpose and feel it down deep in your soul, you keep doing what you're called to do and deal with the consequences however they arise."

"Easy for you to say, Mary. You've chosen to stay in the background. I'm the one putting myself out there."

"We each choose the paths of our own destiny," she calmly replied.

After several more moments lost in thought, especially self-doubt, Josh said, "Well, I do think the message is important to get out in the world and I've made some progress doing so. I guess the path I've chosen is to be the messenger in this time and place. I will continue and just hope I don't later regret that choice."

He walked back toward his office deep in thought about the conversation he would have with Thomas Bartholome and his television appearance.

Chapter 20

The Week Ahead

Early the following Sunday morning, Josh arrived at the TV studio for his live interview with the new local host, Thomas Bartholome. He was greeted warmly by many staff members and shown to the green room to meet with his interviewer.

Thomas greeted Josh a bit cooly saying, "I'm a bit confused why they booked you and asked me to interview you. I've listened to a few of your radio broadcasts and frankly I'm having difficulty getting the point. You don't seem to have any specific agenda and haven't been seeking publicity." He studied Josh for a moment searching for any reaction. "But many in the public have been listening and are intrigued. They want to know more about you, so that will be the focus of our interview. Essentially, who is this Josh Carpenter that is stirring things up?"

Josh replied, "That makes sense. I'm as curious as you are about why I was asked to come on the show. I have been content doing the radio programs with Andrew Fischer and after this will continue to do so. What he told me is that people want to put a face to the person whose voice they hear on his show, and I was asked to do this interview."

"All right," responded Thomas. "We'll keep the focus on who you are and not on the message you claim to be promoting. I just wanted you to know, I have hopes to gain some creds from this new host position but I've had some doubts about this being the best way to get that recognition." He paused. "Let's go into the studio to get things set up and do some video and audio checks."

Josh felt a bit uncomfortable with Thomas's antagonism. It was clear that Thomas wanted to bolster his career and that he thought interviewing Josh might be a stumbling block.

After getting acquainted with the stage and process, Thomas and Josh listened to other anchors give the news reports. With a brief introduction, the cameras switched over to Thomas and Josh sitting in comfortable armchairs, a table between them, each with a mug of coffee in front of them.

"Good morning," began Thomas. "We are here in Chicago today with Josh Carpenter who many have been hearing on the radio along with Andrew Fisher on his program, Can We Talk About It? Many people have been intrigued, positively and negatively, by Josh's commentary and asked us to help put a face on this man, to get to know him. He's been spreading the message 'Don't obscure simple truth' and giving examples where humans have done so throughout history and the various consequences of those actions. He suggests many of those obfuscations are – as he labels them – 'mainly harmless' and suggests his only intent is to 'provoke thoughtfulness.' Interestingly, many people, especially young adults, have embraced those ideas as mottos and memes and we're seeing everything from T-shirts to hoodies to ball caps and bumper stickers. And we're seeing an increasing number of social media posts across many platforms. We're also seeing demonstrations and protests by others who don't like the idea of someone questioning and challenging their beliefs about everything from history to science to politics, including LGBTQ and the environment."

He paused, then clarified. "Today, we're not going to get into Josh's messages and commentary but just try to get a sense of who he is and why he's doing this." He turned to Josh, and prompted, "Tell us a bit about Josh Carpenter."

"I'm not sure there's much to tell," he replied modestly. "My job is what is called big data analysis. We use software algorithms to discover trends and make some predictions based on the past about things to come. Part of my job is to help create and train what many call artificial intelligence engines to sift through mountains of data and produce relevant and usable descriptions in natural language."

"So, you use AI to tell us what's going on and predict the future?" He paused. "Many of us are quite skeptical about letting *artificial* intelligence learn about us and make decisions for us."

"I have similar concerns," said Josh. "I like to think of the 'A' in 'AI' as 'Assistive' rather than 'Artificial'. What these programs do is very real based on whatever data they are fed and asked to sift through. But I think of the output as assisting humans to use *our* intelligence to make sense of the analysis and make human-based decisions about it."

"Interesting. So there still a place for humans to give input and take action. We're not dependent on or controlled by AI," he paused, and added, "Yet."

Before giving Josh a chance to respond, he said, "But we're here today to get to know you, not debate the use and value of AI – however we define it." He looked into the camera briefly then back at Josh. "So, Josh, how did you get into this work?"

"I have always been interested in how we humans solve problems. As I grew up, I often read and watched mysteries, played computer- based adventure games and solved puzzles. I sometimes noticed that I stepped outside of the moment and observed how my mind was working. What facts was I paying attention to? What was I missing? How was I synthesizing what I thought I knew to solve a problem? I was elated when I figured things out – got the right pre-determined answer. But I also enjoyed it when the plot twisted or I was fooled. I wanted to examine what I'd missed or how I'd misled myself. I wanted to better understand how the human brain works to make sense of the world and how we then choose behaviors based on those understandings."

Josh continued. "In my undergraduate studies, I took many classes in psychology and philosophy because I wanted to understand how we think and behave and create belief systems and develop cultures. However, my major was Computer Science, and I was fascinated by the ways we trained computers to gather, record, and report on data. I learned several programming languages from historical ones to the more recent and still evolving relational databases, large language models, and natural language interfaces. In my graduate work, I focused on the developing field of - again, 'artificial' - intelligence, especially about ways we teach our powerful computers to sift through massive data and synthesize it to something meaningful and useful. Computers can do this much faster and more efficiently than humans can, but they can only do their work based on what's fed into them."

"So," suggested Thomas, looking into the camera with a bit of a smirk and trying to get a rise out of Josh, "Does the saying 'Garbage in, Garbage out' apply here as well?"

Josh didn't take the bait. "Absolutely, Thomas. No computer – and no human, for that matter – can take garbage in and be expected to come out with anything but more garbage, even if we choose to believe it's not garbage." He paused. "That's why it's important we all look at what is being fed into our computers – and ourselves – to ensure it's not garbage. That it's not some data that has been unintentionally – or intentionally – manipulated to get to a preferred answer."

Thomas was a bit taken aback. He had expected Josh to be defensive and instead found Josh agreeing with him. He tried to refocus. "So, Josh, your college and post graduate work has been focused on ensuring we don't feed garbage to computers."

"Or ourselves," replied Josh. Then he took a bit more control of the conversation. "Throughout history, humans have looked for patterns in nature hoping to better understand the world and its effect on them. Sometimes it was useful for survival such as following where animals migrated to improve our ability to secure food. Sometimes it was observing the cycles of seasons to know when best to plant various crops. Sometimes humans' proclivity to see patterns occur where there may not have been a pattern to observe. One example that comes to mind is constellations, the belief that heavenly bodies were somehow positioned to depict gods, animals and so forth. Then various characteristics and powers were attributed to these alignments that many people believed had direct influence over their lives."

Thomas started to warm up to the conversation and to Josh. "So, Josh, what's your sign?"

Josh laughed. "See, that's what I mean. It's so easy for us to take these examples, especially those that have been around a very long time, and rather than question the truth behind them, we seriously accept them, or perhaps make light of them. Or in many ways pass them along as if they are true. Some become so common and accepted part of our culture we just continue to perpetuate them. Many of those, perhaps astrology, are mainly harmless. But many other such 'truths' that have been obscured have had more deleterious effects. I'm hopeful to encourage people to examine their beliefs and behaviors to understand where they came from and consider there may be other explanations or perspectives."

"So, are you suggesting that you have the answers?"

"In no way. As Socrates stated, 'The only thing I know for sure is that I don't know anything for sure.' I don't have a special line to truth with a capital T. I only endeavor for myself – and to encourage others – to examine what they do believe, especially when it differs from someone else or is potentially harmful to others or the planet. I only ask that we suspend certainty and be open to other ways of looking at things."

"So, Josh, it sounds like you've been thinking this way for a long time, perhaps even before you went to college. Why are you coming forward now and talking on podcasts and radio shows to spread this message?"

Josh paused, fully aware that he did not want to mention Mary and even less so, Commander. He was wondering the same question that Thomas was asking him.

"When I was about 5 years old, the man I thought of as my dad went to fight in Iraq. He was killed there, and it left me and my mother alone. Mom struggled greatly with the loss and withdrew from everything and everybody. She worked enough at a local dry cleaner to pay the rent and put food on our table, but she kept to herself and enforced me to do the same. I didn't have friends other than my mom. Some of my fondest memories are sitting watching TV with her – especially mysteries. We kept coming up with what we thought were the solutions as the clues were revealed."

Thomas pursued this line of questioning. "Josh, that's interesting. So, were you a momma's boy?"

"No," he replied, again not taking the bait. "I was just a loner but had no problem being alone. I didn't participate in sports or any other extracurricular activities. I kept to myself mostly reading mysteries and doing logic puzzles. I particularly liked reading Sherlock Holmes mysteries and often would enjoy coming up with alternative explanations for the various clues that were uncovered. As I grew older, I discovered several computer games that I could play on my own to solve puzzles. I got hooked on computer adventure stories where a situation was laid out and the user had to solve problems to move up a level or get through to the next challenge. I particularly liked the ones where the player came to a decision point and had to choose which of several alternatives to pursue. How you responded kept changing the game so it could be different each time you played or anyone else played. There was no one right solution, but endless possibilities depending on the choices made along the way. This is what I came to see as a metaphor for life. I would often rethink my choices and wonder what would have happened had I chosen a different path."

Thomas was getting into the background story but he had some other questions he wanted to ask. "Josh, you have a very interesting background, and I can see the connection that led you to the kind of work you do. But I'm still curious – what made you decide to go public with your thinking?"

"My mom worked for over 20 years in a dry cleaning operation. Her continual exposure to some of the chemicals, especially perc, caused her to develop aggressive non-Hodgkin lymphoma. It was quite advanced by the time it was diagnosed but, thankfully, the symptoms were comparatively mild. She passed in a short 18 months.

My mom was my closest friend but also kept me fairly isolated. After she passed away, I felt sad, yet I also had a sense of relief. So, I went for a walk in Millennium Park, then later in Lurie Garden. The sense of freedom was almost overwhelming. And my curiosity was piqued about what I'd been missing. I met Peter Fischer, a Park District employee and botanist. We got to talking about names given to plants and, because of my background and the work I do now, it clicked that we give several different names to the same phenomenon. Peter was a podcaster and asked if he could share these insights on his program, Experiences in the Garden. A few days later he introduced me to his brother, Andrew, the host of the radio show Can We Talk About It? Andrew invited me to be a regular on his program downstairs in this building. We've had numerous very interesting conversations between the two of us and the various guests he's brought in."

"So, do you like having a following?"

"Interesting question, Thomas. I don't think of myself as being a leader of anything. I'm not trying to create a movement, and I'm not seeking or encouraging followers. When you mentioned at the start of this interview that many people, especially young adults have been embracing some of what I've been saying and that others are protesting the same, honestly, I've been unaware. I come each week to talk with Andrew and his guests to have thoughtful conversations. I have no idea who else or how many others are listening. As someone recently asked me – 'Hey man. Do you live in a cave?' – I think I might, but my cave is simply doing my job, commuting to my home, and occasionally walking in the park."

"Some have accused you of being a gadfly – someone who is annoying and constantly questioning people's politics and beliefs."

"Well – I guess I could be a gadfly in many senses – but my intent is not to annoy anyone. As I've said, my intent is to provoke thoughtfulness. By that I mean encourage people to consider where their ideas and beliefs come from and to do it in a way that also considers the impacts of those ideas and beliefs on their own behaviors and how they might affect other people and the planet. In other words, to challenge their own thinking and that of others with kindness and openness."

"Well Josh, our time is almost up, and I must say it's been eye-opening for me. I had assumed you were a man on a mission and were looking for publicity to draw in more supporters. Now I experience you as a genuinely curious, humble man – perhaps even a bit reticent – just asking us to consider where our ideas come from and how they affect our behaviors. And you seem to do this in a gentle, non- judgmental manner. So, what's next for you?"

"Well, Andrew and I have another session coming up about the role of religion throughout history and the effects today, some of which are mainly harmless. But we'll also consider the possibility that some religious beliefs and practices affecting us today may be based on simple truths that have been obscured for various reasons. It should be very interesting."

Thomas turned to the camera. "Well listeners. I hope you have enjoyed getting to know a little about the man behind the message. You can hear more from him on …" and Thomas provided the call numbers for the radio broadcast and passed the program back to the news anchors.

Chapter 21

Religion

"And a good Sunday morning to all our listeners out there," began Andrew. "I understand that we now have about 1.5 million followers who are tuning in to this live broadcast or the streaming platforms to listen to the recorded programs. I am amazed and humbled by your participation. I guess many of you are listening now because we are continuing our conversations with Josh Carpenter, a big data analyst who has become a spokesperson spreading the message – Don't obscure simple truth."

He continued. "For those of you who haven't listened to the entire series, I offer this brief recap. Over the past several weeks Josh and I and a few guests have discussed things related to names of plants, to U.S. history related to indigenous populations and westward expansion, to current civil rights issues, to government and politics. In every case Josh has asked questions that, in his words, 'provoke thoughtfulness' encouraging us to ask some challenging questions about where our ideas and beliefs come from and how, throughout history for several reasons, the simple truths that underpin much of our society, have been obscured intentionally or unintentionally. He has suggested that some of those obfuscations haven't seemed to have a big negative consequence. They are as he says, 'mainly harmless'. He has further encouraged us to 'suspend certainty' when it seems our thoughts and actions are significantly different from someone else's. To put aside our beliefs and carefully examine our own thinking and that of others to determine where and how we adopted those beliefs."

After a pause, "And today we're going to talk about religion, some of the earliest creations of community beliefs up to present-day religious experiences, beliefs, and actions. So, sit *forward* while Josh provokes thoughtfulness for all of us. Josh, anything you want to add before we introduce our guests?"

Josh immediately replied. "Thanks Andrew. The most important thing I want to emphasize is that I have no special knowledge or experience to suggest what is true and how we should act. I'm just a guy, probably not that different from many of our listeners, who is curious about why we think and act the way we do and how that thinking impacts other people and the planet. The only difference is possibly that I've taken on a responsibility to ask questions of myself and others publicly to raise doubts and help us each examine the roots of our thinking."

Andrew stepped in. "And that's why today's conversation may be extremely challenging. We're going to talk about the foundational roots of our thinking about religion, including beliefs about whether and what regarding a supreme being – and how those beliefs inspire us to behave." He paused. "And to help us work through some of these questions, we have three wise men and one wise woman with many years of experience. Again, since our program is primarily intended for the U.S. audience, we're going to focus on the U.S."

Andrew continued with introductions. "Today we have Michael O'Reilly, a minister at a mega-church outside of Chicago representing the roughly two-thirds of Americans who identify with some sect of Christianity. Next we have Anita Morehead, a prolific writer in the secular space representing views of the second largest group, the slightly less than one-third of Americans who identify as unaffiliated or 'nones' including atheists, non-religious, and agnostic. Next, we have Samuel Rosenschein, a rabbi of Reform Judaism to share perspectives from the 2% of the population who identify as religious Jews. And we have Omar Ali representing the fast-growing Muslim population comprising just under 2% of the U.S. population who follow Islam. Lady and gentlemen, thank you for joining us today."

Each guest nodded and responded that they were glad to be a part of today's conversation.

Josh kicked things off. "I'd like to start with this question: What is the purpose of religion?"

"I'd like to start if I may," stated Michael. The others nodded, so he continued. "I think any religion intends to provide its followers with answers to big questions. What is the meaning of life and death? Where is our place in the universe? Are we alone or what else is there? I think religion helps people feel some kind of spiritual connection to something outside ourselves."

"I agree with that," continued Omar. "In addition, religion provides moral and ethical guidance to help us as individuals and collectively make choices and take actions that are good for maintaining a sense of belonging. Common values help shape laws, customs, and traditions that govern societies."

"I agree with both of you," added Samuel. "And would add that religion encourages compassion, love, and service to others. And religious beliefs offer reassurance in times of suffering, loss and uncertainty. Further, I think religion fosters a sense of belonging through shared stories and traditions."

Anita spoke up. "I agree with much of what you three have said, except perhaps for Michael's suggestion about the connection to something outside ourselves. I'm sure we'll come back to that point. The other concept I'd add to our list about a possible purpose for religion is through practices like prayer, meditation and fasting to cultivate self-control, humility, and inner peace. However, like many of the 'nones', I think we humans can meet all of the purposes we listed without the structure of religion."

"So let me see if I got this correct," said Josh. "From what all of you said, whether it's within a religious structure or not, humans seek answers to big existential questions, some kind of spiritual connection whether inside or outside oneself. We want clarity and guidance about moral questions – what the right action is to take in any given situation. We want a sense of belonging perhaps through the experience of feeling connected to a shared history and set of practices. We want comfort and reassurances through situations of suffering and uncertainty. And we practice disciplines that help us individually or collectively find inner peace and be of loving service to others. Did I get all that?"

There were nods all around.

For the next 90 minutes, Josh asked other questions, and the guests asked some of their own. They all agreed that religious and non- religious movements often start with a single leader – a founder – who attracts followers who help spread their messages. In the three religions, there are claims that the founder and some followers were spoken to directly by their supreme entity or its supporting staff. For the non-religious, there were many thinkers and writers whose ideas were propagated. They further agreed that stories were told or written about these founders, sometimes hundreds of years later, that may have embellished the truth or obscured it.

Also, stories vary widely about the historical Jesus – whether he was the prophesied messiah, whether he performed miracles as told in the New Testament, the whole story surrounding his birth, his relationship to God, and his death. Christians obviously believe in his crucifixion and resurrection three days later. For Muslims, the Quran talks about Jesus as being miraculously born to a virgin, performing miracles, and being a Muslim, meaning he submitted to God's will. Muslims do not believe Jesus was the son of God or that he was crucified but was taken up to God and not killed. All three religions believe in some final judgment and that the messiah will come either the first time or on a return engagement. Non-religious people talk about the historical Jesus as only a human, a teacher, and a moral philosopher, focusing on his teachings and actions rather than his divinity or religious significance. There was a tense discussion about the historical Jesus, an Aramaic Jew in the Middle East, who is often depicted in the U.S. as a white male with blond hair and blue eyes.

The discussion also explored the numerous times there were schisms in any given religion and the times they were a war with each other. They agreed that as leadership changes and time passes, their religions adapt to the context of the times and cultures. Josh suggested that these various iterations in some way might obscure the simple truths with which the religions began. Anita suggested that the continual scientific discoveries provided new ways to explain the previously unknown truths about the origins of the universe and human beings place in it.

There were questions about the existence and character of a supreme being. They acknowledged in each of the three religions there were over 100 names for this being, while Anita reiterated that non- religious people avoid the word 'God' or any entity as a deity. They discussed that over the ages, many theologians and philosophers, nonreligious ones as well, endeavored to prove the existence of a single supreme being. There have been at least 36 so-called proofs for the existence of such a being, yet they all agreed that even the proofs that claimed to be based only on reason and logic, the bottom line was they all took a leap of faith in their final acceptance of the existence or non-existence of such a being.

They had all agreed that one purpose of religion was to provide ethical guidance and laws that ensured society would survive and thrive. Some laws were a bit vague leaving lots of room for interpretation and adaptation to changing context and new learnings. Perhaps some of these were related to dietary guidance for health reasons or beliefs about the sanctity of certain animals. Other laws were guidance about clothing and appearance in public related to showing that someone was a part of a specific community or gender. Some laws were much more specific and even detailed consequences of breaking a given law. There was debate about whether these laws were passed down by divine commandment or man-made. For example, some of the religious and secular texts took the law about "an eye for an eye" to be a guide for justice and fairness, others as guidance for retribution, and others that vengeance is the province of God, not humans. Still others took the concepts quite literally.

Josh asked, "How would you describe the effect of religious or non- religious beliefs and practices on government and politics?"

Michael jumped in. "The United States is predominantly a Christian nation. As stated earlier, over 2/3 of Americans identify with some Christian denomination. That means most of the people who vote in our democracy are Christian and our sense of right and wrong has the greatest influence on who is elected, the passing and enforcement of laws, and the general ethos of the society."

Samuel suggested, "I think Michael's right for better or worse. However Judaism has contributed to establishing political authority and reinforcing social hierarchies by our involvement in legal systems, helping to establish societal norms and ethics, and work toward human equality. The majority of Jews in the U.S. support a Democratic agenda and lean liberal, however there is also strong right-wing pro-Israel support."

"Muslims take different approaches to political involvement," offered Omar. "Some Muslims resist political participation, proposing the separation of governance based on Islamic norms and non-Islamic governance. After strong anti-Muslim sentiments arose in America following September 11, 2001, many of us chose to participate in politics to debunk stereotypes, to fight against hate, and to promote social inclusion and civic engagement."

Anita responded, "We non-religious people see both positive and negative influences of religion on government and politics. We think there should be no religious influence in politics and government that is not based on logic and reason. It's interesting to note that phrases like 'In God We Trust', 'One Nation Under God', and 'God Bless America' seem to permeate many of our political speeches, loyalty oaths and even our currency. We support a secular form of government."

The examples and debate on this influence continued for a few more minutes. Especially difficult were comments and questions about whether politicians, especially party leaders derived their power through some kind of divine authority, directly or through support of religious movements.

Josh commented, "I find it interesting how much of your stories overlap, although with some important differences. Going back to the mostly-agreed-upon ideas about the purpose of religion, I'm curious. Where do you think we get our ideas about religion or non-religion?"

Anita started this time. "For younger people, I'm speaking about children here, many get their ideas from their family or other adult influences. Childhood socialization is powerful especially when introduced early in life when the brain is not fully formed, and the child is most susceptible to training and indoctrination."

Samuel responded, "That's probably true, Anita, but I think a bit harsh. Families and communities whether faith-driven or otherwise, have cultural traditions that guide them on common beliefs and behaviors, especially around what's right and what's wrong. These communities also reinforce their norms through education, celebrations or recognitions of meaningful historical events and people – their shared history – that keeps the stories alive and engaging."

"And in many families and communities," interjected Michael, "children are exposed to music, and movement which are often even more memorable than the stories. Children sing and dance and recite words, often in languages other than their predominant tongue, that get embedded in how they think and behave. As children and adults age, they are also influenced by media and literature that reinforce their earlier learning."

"And," Omar added, "rituals such as attending a place of worship and participating in prayer and acts of devotion further reinforces their learning and behavior."

"And sometimes," suggested Anita, "as people mature they are exposed to different ways of thinking. They may begin to question what they've been taught about a supreme being or religion, what they've learned of science, and what they've personally experienced and they move toward agnosticism or even atheism. Many of the religious teachings from their youth just don't seem to make sense anymore or withstand their questioning. What someone chooses to believe or not believe becomes much more of a reasoned and individual response."

"Very interesting," responded Josh. "Again, I sense more commonality than difference here. I'll suggest that no matter how one comes to believe whatever it is they accept as true, it may be so deeply ingrained as to not be questioned. Or if it is questioned, it can lead a person to a different set of conclusions and behaviors." He paused to note they all seemed to agree, up to a point. "Further," he continued, "For most people, whatever they believe and how they got there may be less important than how that determination leads to their behaviors. Many, whether identifying as religious or nonreligious live by a golden rule – to do unto others as they would have done unto themselves. Or more specifically, to practice kindness, compassion, patience, humility, gentleness, and forgiveness. I think these behaviors are good for humanity and the planet." He paused and once again sensed mostly agreement. He continued, "And it's when we decide – consciously or unconsciously – to try to enforce our particular beliefs onto others, especially how they influence politicians and government, we may move into trouble that is not mainly harmless."

Andrew, who'd been mostly quietly listening, jumped in to announce, "This has been fascinating discussion and there is so much more to explore. Unfortunately, we have come to the end of our allotted time for today. I want to thank our four guests and Josh for their joint efforts to provoke thoughtfulness today. I truly appreciate each person's willingness to suspend certainty and listen closely to what every other person chose to share" He paused. "To our listeners, thank you for tuning in. Please let us know what comments you have and any questions you would like us to pursue in future broadcasts. We look forward to hearing from you."

And with that, the program ended.

Chapter 22

Mixed Reactions

A few days later Josh heard from Andrew that they needed to talk. They arranged to meet at a coffee shop just down the street from Josh's workplace.

Andrew told Josh that the station had received numerous comments and questions. "Most comments express appreciation that the show is stimulating a lot of thinking and deeper conversations with others. Many say they are suspending certainty to listen to people, especially those of different backgrounds, beliefs, and behaviors. There is an increase in compassion."

He continued. "Some suggested other questions or deeper dives into some of the topics already explored, possibly with other guests. The programs on climate change and human impacts on the environment, race, politics and religion are of particular interest for further exploration."

Andrew went on. "One frequently asked question is about Josh himself. Listeners wanted to know where you got your ideas and what else you're thinking. And now the owners of our station want you to do another live interview with Bartholome to share more about Josh, the person."

Josh reiterated to Andrew, "This is not about me. It's about spreading the message – 'Do not obscure simple truth'. It is not a personal effort to be a leader of any kind of movement." But after a bit of back-and-forth, Josh acknowledged that he did have some thoughts he might like to share and agreed to a follow-up.

"There are two other categories of responses you should know about," suggested Andrew. "There were many hundreds of responses with words of encouragement to keep doing what you're doing. Some people admitted to following you closely and trying to emulate your style of provoking thoughtfulness. All kinds of social and printed media are talking about you and this program. And in addition to wearing apparel with your various statements, some have come to carry signs or wear clothing with the letters 'WWJD' meaning 'What Would Josh Do?' You've started something whether you wanted to or not."

Josh just shook his head. "I don't get it. A lot of this just sounds like more ways to obscure simple truth." He paused. "You mentioned there was another category of responses."

"Yes," stated Andrew with all seriousness. "There were a substantial number of negative comments and even threats against you and this station. People are saying that you are disruptive, undermining the status quo, challenging the value of religious beliefs, and so on. They say you're an agitator and stirring up hate. They suggest that you're in it for yourself trying to start a rebellion." He paused. "Josh, I think you need to take this seriously. Some people have it out for you. Perhaps we should get a security detail to keep an eye on you."

Josh laughed. "You can't be serious – or they can't. I haven't made any suggestions about the way things should be. I've stated that I have no answers. I only have questions and want to better understand what some simple truths are and how they have been obscured over time for whatever reasons. I have no agenda other than to encourage examination of our own ideas and beliefs."

Andrew responded and gently touched his hand to Josh's shoulder. "You and I know that. But this has grown way beyond the two of us having a philosophical bull session. It's affecting people, strongly, in many ways, some of which may be dangerous."

Josh blinked and shook his head. "I'll think about it and what, if anything, I might do differently. Thanks for letting me know."

And with that, Josh walked out of the coffee shop and returned to work.

Chapter 23

The Attack

Mary had noticed more people, especially young people, walking through the park wearing caps, sweatshirts, hoodies, and T-shirts with various quotes attributable to Josh. She became concerned when she also saw some people wearing the slogan 'WWJD' or carrying signs with the same letters, some with a picture of Josh captured from the TV screen from his interview a couple weeks ago. She overheard people talking about how important he and his message had become in their lives.

She was both proud and worried. As she sat on her park bench surrounded by pigeons, she heard Commander in her head and read his and others' droppings. They too were concerned. Was the message getting out there? For sure. But the focus was more on Josh than on the message. They believed that they were not mutually exclusive, but were worried that if something happened to Josh, the message would get lost. They agreed they would keep an eye on Josh and do whatever they could to ensure his safety.

For his part, Josh was deeply bothered by what Andrew had told him about the responses. He again told himself that this wasn't about him. At the same time he acknowledged that he couldn't control how people responded. He wasn't trying to start or lead a movement of any sort, but it was happening nevertheless. And, on the other hand, there were many people very upset with who they thought he was and what he was doing. They wanted to, at best, discredit him and belittle his efforts or, at worst, cause him harm. He was at a loss what to do and decided that perhaps Commander and Mary might have some ideas. So, he headed to the park.

As he was walking through the park in search of Mary, he noticed several people wearing apparel and carrying WWJD signs with his photo. Fortunately, he'd worn a baseball cap himself and had some sunglasses with him. He put on the glasses and pulled down the cap hoping to pass unobserved.

What he didn't notice was a small group of people who had followed him from his office and were now trailing him through the park. These were people who didn't like his message and were strongly against what seemed to be happening as a result. Most were connected to an organization with a particular religious and political viewpoint that felt threatened by what Josh was saying. They ignored his humility and statements of having no answers. They and others had numerous postings on various social media sites suggesting all kinds of things about Josh. Some dug up information about his mother, Mary, having been suspected of child abuse. They shared the fact that he was a bastard and suggested the man pretending to be his father couldn't stand him or his mother, so went off to war. Others talked about how he was a loner who spent most of his time alone with his mother or on his computer doing who knows what. The innuendos were not subtle. Other posts suggested his work with big data and AI were designed to give control to computers and take away human jobs and even take over the government. It was nonstop fake news, but it gathered an ever-increasing number of followers. Some of those followers were walking behind Josh in the park intending to harm his person.

As Josh spotted Mary off to the side of the Bean, the group following him neared. All of a sudden, pigeons seemingly from everywhere rose frantically flapping their wings and pooping on the heads of the group following Josh. Other people in that area of the park were panicked by the disruption and started racing everywhere to get away from the mess.

Mary waved Josh over but with a motion indicated he should just walk by. "You were being followed. You are in danger. Don't seek me out again for a while. I'll get a message to you when it's safe again."

Josh took the hint and kept walking. He circled down to Michigan Avenue to be among the crowd of pedestrians and made his way back up Randolph Street to his office. By the time he got to his cubicle, he was perspiring heavily and shaking like a leaf. He was overwhelmed with fear and confused by whatever was going on.

He took some calming breaths and after a few minutes felt his heart rate was back to normal. "But," he thought to himself, "what I'm doing must be important because it's causing all these strong responses. Perhaps doing the TV interview will help to calm the concerns people have as I reinforce that I have no answers, only observations and questions." He called the station to confirm his willingness for a follow-up with Thomas Bartholome and to be live next Sunday morning.

Chapter 24

What Was Josh Thinking?

This time was different. Thomas Bartholome met Josh in the Green Room and warmly welcomed him back to the show. "Josh, I've got to say I'm thrilled to have you back. The ratings from the last show have been extremely strong and our sponsors expect even higher marks this time." He paused. "I admit I was a bit put off last time by the request to interview you, but by the end, I was very comfortable listening to you share your history. I am looking forward to going deeper in today's program."

"I did notice you seemed to have a bit of an attitude at the beginning of the last program," smiled Josh. "I thought we had a good conversation and I'm glad to be here again with you. I'm not sure exactly what you want to talk about, but I have a few ideas I prepared to share with your viewers."

"That sounds great, Josh. Our general theme based on audience responses is to learn more about how you developed your ideas and what else you are thinking about."

"Sounds good. Thank you, Thomas."

They moved into the same studio they were in before. The same chairs and tables along with fresh cups of coffee. As last time, there was a brief news update and then the cameras went live.

Facing the camera, Thomas opened with, "Good morning viewers. We are excited to have a return visit from Josh Carpenter, the man who is stirring up some public interest while spreading the message – 'Don't obscure simple truth'. Last time we spoke, Josh gave us some insight to who he is as a person and why he's on this mission. Today we want to learn more about how Josh developed some of his ideas and what else he's thinking about." Thomas turned to face Josh and again welcomed him to the show.

"Josh, why don't we start with another brief review of your background and how your ideas developed?"

"Thank you, Thomas. I'm honored to be back with you and to have this opportunity to share some of my thinking. However, I want to strongly emphasize again that I am no one special. I've had no visitation from a supreme being, no time alone in a cave or out in the desert, no burning bushes. My only quest, as I've said before, is to provoke thoughtfulness – to encourage each of us to gain clarity on where our ideas and beliefs come from, what is the simple truth that underlies our experience and to examine how our beliefs impact our behavior and the effects that has on others and the planet. I am a curious observer and ask questions to encourage that self-examination. I repeat – I have no special knowledge. I do not give advice other than self-examination. And I do not seek any kind of leadership or a following."

"Pretty strong statement there, Josh" responded Thomas.

"Yes. I felt that it was needed because I'm hearing and seeing people dressed in slogans, carrying signs and arguing with others who hold different views. This is the exact opposite of what I was hoping would happen. Slogans and signs either agreeing or disagreeing with what I'm saying are possibly examples of people obscuring simple truths. I want to encourage self-examination and to have people listen with curiosity and kindness to one another. That is the way to raise our levels of knowledge, mutual acceptance, and care for each other."

"That sounds like a good point to segway to how you came to that idea."

"Thomas, last time I was here I mentioned I had taken some classes in psychology in my undergraduate studies. One concept I keep coming back to – admittedly with my own spin on it – is theories about human development. Two things stand out to me in this arena. First, there are three distinct domains within which people understand a situation and make decisions that determine their behaviors. Those three domains are moral, social-conventional, and personal. Simply put, reasoning in the moral domain as suggested by Lawrence Kohlberg recognizes rules that are universal and unchanging. This would include such things as not killing people and not stealing."

Thomas interjected. "Sounds like much of what is specified in the Bible and Quran."

"There is much overlap and concurrence," Josh continued. "Reasoning in the social-conventional domain as posited by Elliot Turiel is about rules, or perhaps we should call them guidelines. How do we reason and act when we think things are more mutable and change depending on the context of social norms, culture, and the times? Examples of such guidelines might include how we dress, what we eat, where we live.

"So, a bit more flexible, then, right?"

"It might seem so, I'll come back to that." He paused. "Reasoning in the personal domain as explored by Larry Nucci suggests that there are some guidelines and practices that are only about choices made by an individual. Reasoning and making choices in the personal domain might include how I wear my hair, what media I choose to pay attention to, and who I choose as my friends."

"Got it. Three domains. But as I listen to you, I can see where we might blur the lines a bit."

"Exactly, Thomas. And that's my first point. Depending on who is doing the reasoning, there may be some ideas they think have a moral context and are inflexible. Another person may think the same ideas are not moral but require decisions from the social context alone. And yet another person may think the same situation calls for only a personal decision."

"Can you give us an example?" suggested Thomas.

"Here's a rough example regarding the continuation of a pregnancy. Some people consider this a moral issue and claim that there is a moral obligation to see a pregnancy to term, almost no matter what. Someone else may argue that the decision about giving birth or having a pregnancy terminated has changed over time and is more dependent on the social norms of the time and place being considered. And still someone else may say the decision is a personal one to be made by the pregnant person along with any doctor or significant others she may choose to involve in her decision."

"I think I understand. It's about which domain someone is using for their reasoning to make whatever decision. And awareness of which domain leads to all kinds of arguments for or against whatever decision."

"Exactly. And again, I'm not suggesting any specific answer, but suggesting a deeper understanding of ways we might obscure simple truths can help us have more productive conversations about the basis of our ideas or beliefs, and therefore the decisions we make and our behaviors."

"Josh, earlier you suggested there was another idea that you wanted to share about this research in human development and domain theory."

"Thank you, Thomas. Some researchers suggest that our maturity of reasoning in each of these domains is not a direct linear path. They suggest that a person's reasoning in a given domain may suffice for a time, but that faced with new situations requiring different choices, they come to a place where the previous level of reasoning seems inadequate to accommodate all the variables. They may then go through a stage of rejecting their previous beliefs as insufficient and, as yet not have a clarity on what might be a more comprehensive way of looking at the situation."

"I've experienced something like that myself a few times," offered Thomas. "One that comes to mind was my parents giving me a curfew when I was old enough to drive and started dating. They laid down the law, perhaps just social norms, and I initially followed their wishes. Later I felt I could make my own decisions about when to come home, so I ignored their rules. I rejected their rules. I was immediately given consequences that enforced me to follow their rules. Eventually we made compromises, and I had more freedom within broader guidelines."

"Your example does demonstrate what many people go through in their maturation process. As children we behave in ways that we're told we should, either for moral or socially conventional reasons. As we grow, some of us feel those rules no longer serve us well, so we push back against them until, through some process, we come to a more workable understanding. That more workable understanding itself may be challenged again at a later point and bring about yet another desire to push back.

"That makes sense" agreed Thomas.

"And," added Josh, "My observations suggest this happens with groups of people not just individuals. We can see it in families, communities, religious groups, political groups and so on. Some ideas and beliefs are accepted as the right or normal way of thinking, and then the group starts to experience some ideas and behaviors that aren't working as well as they used to, and they push back on past ways of thinking."

"Yes, I can see that as well," agreed Thomas.

"And one further observation," added Josh. "Several theorists and my own experience suggest that an individual or group may stop this process at some point. They either believe that they are right and accept what they believe, or they push back on anyone or any other group that seems to challenge them." He paused. "And that leads me to another idea I learned about a few years ago. Groupthink."

"I've heard of that," responded Thomas enthusiastically. Josh got the sense that Thomas wanted his viewers to see him as more than just an interviewer. That he had some useful knowledge and experience to share as well.

So, Josh, wanting to support Thomas, asked, "What do you know about groupthink?"

"I believe it's when a group of people seem to be thinking about a situation the same way. It's like they are of one mind."

"Absolutely," agreed Josh. "And Irving Janis who defined groupthink, suggests it has a set of characteristics that, at least to me, can seem a bit disturbing. The group prioritizes conformity and harmony over critical thinking and rational decision-making. Members of the group consider themselves to be invulnerable and to have a high degree of moral righteousness. Any *outside* individual or group is derided and belittled. Anyone *in* the group experiences strong peer pressure to go along with the rest of the group, even if they might disagree. The group wants to give the impression of unanimity. And to my way of thinking, the most dangerous part of groupthink is the group's belief that their leader is infallible. They are to be followed without question."

"Wow!" uttered Thomas. "There's a lot more to groupthink than I had considered. As I look around our society, I see a number of people in groups that might have some of these characteristics. What immediately comes to mind are groups with political agendas, or religious affiliations, and..." He took a breath. "This almost sounds like a cult or even a totalitarian political ideology."

Josh responded. "Let's be careful of how we describe things. We can identify many instances where groupthink exists and may be dangerous. There are other examples where it may be mainly harmless. My suggestion for each of us again is to be curious observers. Try not to be prejudiced or judgmental but to provoke thoughtfulness through our own self-examination and by asking questions and deeply listening to people's responses."

"That sounds like good advice, Josh. Did you have something else to add?"

"Yes. In some ways similar to groupthink, is the idea of a dominant narrative. This is the case in which a story or idea is widely accepted and shapes society's understanding and public discourse. The dominant narrative often reinforces the interests and perspectives of those in power, even if it is not based on reality."

"Can you give us a few examples?" Thomas requested.

"Sure. They range from ideas that are probably mainly harmless to others that are very dangerous. One mainly harmless practice, in my opinion, is automatic responses in various situations. For example, when we greet someone we automatically ask 'How are you?' sometimes as just another way of saying 'hello'. Or when we depart, someone might automatically say 'Have a nice day' as another way of simply saying 'goodbye'."

Thomas chuckled. "Yeah, I do that. Or when someone sneezes, automatically saying 'God bless you' even if it's directed to someone who is a nonbeliever."

"That one has several interesting connections," agreed Josh. "A more challenging example of dominant narratives comes from biologists who study animal behavior. Some of their earlier descriptions are now being questioned, but it's interesting to see how they emerged. For example, some researchers stated that Canada Geese and Sandhill Cranes mate for life. Also, some suggested that most animal species are binary having distinctly male or female characteristics and behaviors. Such scientific descriptions supported the dominant narrative and were used to emphasize desired behaviors among humans. More current research is demonstrating that there are lots of exceptions. For example, Bonobos, apes closely related to humans, have been observed having same-sex interactions between both males and females. Male Bottlenose Dolphins have been observed engaging in sexual activity with one another. These ideas are examples of people obscuring simple truths because of intent to support the dominant narrative about human sexual behavior.

"Those narratives seem more provocative than 'Have a nice day'," suggested Thomas.

"Perhaps, Thomas. We can see how such a dominant narrative affects how we talk about and treat LGBTQ people today. And there are some people in power now who want us to acknowledge that there are only two genders – male and female – even in light of the gender diversity that we can observe daily."

"That is truly a hot button these days," exclaimed Thomas.

"More challenging narratives bring up questions of ethnicity and race, global warming, territorial and political conflicts. In many of these cases, the dominant narrative espoused by people on different sides of the situation may evolve into groupthink, making it even more difficult to have productive dialogue." He paused and took a sip of his coffee. "We humans seem to want things to be a certain way. It eases our discomfort and allows us to believe that reality is predictable and possibly controllable. We have ideas about the way things are until and unless proven otherwise. I think of these ideas as theories in use. They are not necessarily right or complete, but we accept that they're working for us at least for now."

"I like that," suggested Thomas. "'Theories in use'. It seems to allow us to get on with life without the constant questioning of what's real, what does it all mean. If we were constantly questioning everything, I think it would be chaos. The human race would probably stagnate."

"That's the rub," agreed Josh. "What should we accept as a workable theory in use, especially if it seems to be mainly harmless? And when should we look deeper at the origins and maneuverings of our beliefs and question their validity? For some scientists, as an example, they do experiments as a way of supporting what we think is real or challenging us to consider different possibilities. In olden times, the dominant narratives suggested that the Earth was the center of the universe, that the world was flat, or, as some still question, that human beings evolved from other species. More recently theories and research such as concepts of relativity and time, how gravity and light bend as they travel through space and developing theories of quantum mechanics are challenging some of the dominant narratives, especially in physics. Other experiments, such as those trying to determine whether light moves as particles or in waves seem to suggest it depends on the tools we use to observe and measure. What might be the implications and opportunities that arise as we think in new ways?"

Josh paused again. "I think in some ways a lot of this informs us about the development of AI and big data analysis. Last time you and I talked, you mentioned the challenge of garbage in, garbage out. Perhaps we can see it more broadly today. My work focuses on trying to separate the dominant narratives about intelligence, specifically computer intelligence, from what is fundamental and provable. AI is vastly different from traditional computer programming. With traditional computing, programs and applications are built around very definitive logic structures and processes. The programs dictate how the input data is handled and what the output should be. With AI, it's about training for pattern recognition and is more analogous to how the human brain works. There is no predetermined way AI handles inputs and produces outputs. Depending on the large language models used in their training, different AI systems can produce very different output, just as different humans exposed to similar situations may have different sense of what is going on. That is why I think of AI as 'assistive intelligence' rather than 'artificial intelligence'. It means we humans still must choose what and how we ask questions and how we interpret and act on the results."

Josh continued. "My colleagues and I recognize that much of what we consider in our analysis is interpreted in light of what we want reality to be and perhaps unconsciously we predetermine the answers we suspect or desire. We obscure simple truths to fit our paradigms."

Thomas was aware that their time today was coming to an end. "Josh, we are almost out of time today, and I have found this conversation to be extremely thought provoking. I hope we can have you back again to pursue this further. For now, do you have any last words?"

"I've enjoyed it as well, Thomas. My hope is that we've provoked thoughtfulness, and others will make opportunities to dive deeper into their own thinking and that of others." He paused and looked directly at the camera. "And again, I want to emphasize that I am just a curious observer and a nonjudgmental questioner. I have no special knowledge. I am not the leader of any movement, nor do I seek personal followers. The ability to observe, question, and clarify is open to anyone who chooses that path."

Thomas concluded the program thanking Josh with an invitation to his viewers to submit comments and questions and tune in for further radio broadcasts at his sister station.

As the cameras were shut off, Thomas and Josh stood and shook hands. Thomas again thanked Josh for the stimulating conversation and likelihood of high ratings. As they left, Thomas chuckled and said, "Have a nice day."

Chapter 25

Destiny

Mary was deep in thought. She sensed that Josh's efforts to spread the message had somehow become obscured by people seeing him as the leader or figurehead of a movement. She feared for his safety as he had stirred up some strong reactions and was seen as disruptive to the status quo.

Her understanding through communication and interpretations of Commander's droppings and telepathy was that Josh may have unintentionally become more important than the message. She understood that anyone could be an emissary of the lost message. She grasped that her destiny demanded that she keep trying to recruit others.

She was extremely grateful that Josh had found out about the demise of her previous employer, Flash, Flesh and Fantasy. She was relieved that her fear of being found by her old boyfriend and his fellow immoral cops was no longer a possibility. And even though she had now chosen, or been chosen, for this new life, she felt she could go back to using her real name, Corrine Randall. Her consideration was partially based on her conversations with Josh in which they discussed how the names we give things, and ourselves, are sometimes a way we obscure simple truths. She wanted to be more authentic and was thankful to Josh for helping her realize that.

As she considered these ideas, she also wondered if these ideas about the message and her search for others to spread the word were really from Commander or just in her own head. She'd been hiding out and pretending to be a bag lady for so long she wasn't sure if she had her head on straight. "But," she thought, "even if it's all in my own head, it seems to be important and working to spread the word, wherever it comes from. Josh has been particularly exceptional in sharing this lost message. But he can't do it alone. I have to try to find others to help."

She got up off her bench, took firm hold of her pushcart, and began walking around the park looking for potential messengers. Commander and his fellow pigeons flitted from space to space moving along with her.

Josh left the studio after the morning's broadcast. Once again, he was deep in thought reflecting on the conversation he'd just completed with Thomas. His mind was ablaze with all kinds of further ideas he'd had over time that seemed to be coming together, and he was anxious to share more with Andrew the following week on the radio broadcast. "Humans are very creative," he thought. "We can make stuff up simply by combining words and concepts. One idea I have is to combine "cognitive" and "kinetic" to invent a new word – "cognetics" – the process of moving from thought to action. And we can describe something like a purple giraffe with antlers and even make images of those invented things. Or we can make up a story about a time long ago when extraterrestrials visited the Earth and seeded it with our human ancestors. Or perhaps even a story about someone who was the son of god and performed miracles, then was crucified and resurrected. The more seemingly possible and the longer the story has been around, the more we humans seem to accept it as true. I wonder."

He continued walking back toward his office heading south along Michigan Avenue near the north end of Millennium Park. He turned and walked east up the small rise that was Randolph Street approaching his office, still deep in thought.

"And the way politics seems to be happening in our country now," he thought to himself. "We are so divided and divisive. Some people in power seem to have redefined the concept of a bully pulpit. It used to be that it served people in power to have an amplified voice to persuade their followers to follow their lead. Now it seems the concept has a much stronger influence on the 'bully' part, belittling and attacking people who don't agree with them. Groupthink in its most dangerous version, especially about the infallibility of the leader and the unwillingness to question them."

As he neared the top of the hill in front of the Aon Center, he thought he would seek out Mary and Commander again to ask for their input and guidance. He looked both ways and walked out to the median and stood on the curb waiting for the traffic to clear and allow him to cross over to the park.

Suddenly and without a sound, an east-bound electric vehicle jumped the curb and struck Josh head-on. The vehicle, built like a tank, quickly completed a U-turn and headed west back toward Michigan Avenue. It soon disappeared into traffic.

Josh lay across the median. His arms were outstretched and his legs crossed and twisted from the collision. His lifeless eyes seemed to be looking at the sky and the expression on his face was one of bewilderment about what had happened.

Witnesses stopped traffic and rushed to his side. Several people called 911. A few tried to take pictures of the retreating vehicle, but it didn't have a license plate and was soon lost in the traffic.

Police and EMTs were quick to arrive. Josh was examined and pronounced dead at the scene. Witness interviews led the police to suspect it was an intentional hit-and-run, especially since several witnesses reported seeing the vehicle jump the curb and aim directly at the pedestrian.

EMTs and the police recovered identification and determined that the downed pedestrian was Josh Carpenter. After several hours of further investigation, Josh's body had been covered with a sheet and taken to the morgue. It would probably take at least three days for the police to review recordings from any area cameras and try to identify the perpetrator. It was clear that Josh was dead and his mission to spread the lost message was summarily ended.

Across the street in the park, many people had gathered to watch the investigation. Among them was a woman dressed in a dark overcoat with a torn right sleeve. She had on a pair of old Reeboks with a hole in the right sole. She was draped with a red scarf wrapped loosely around the upturned collar of her coat. She seemed to be in shock and just stood there shaking her head. After a while, she pulled her cart with its wobbly back wheel and walked away with tears in her eyes. She found a place to sit and soon was surrounded by a few pigeons walking near her and making a mess with their droppings. She sighed heavily and realized it was time to get on with her mission to find others to spread the message.

So, Corrine Randall sits on a park bench in active pursuit of her destiny.

Author's Note

I hope The Lost Message stimulated some thinking.

Many of my early readers shared that The Lost Message provoked their own thoughtfulness. They suggested the book lends itself to further discussion such as in a book group. I created a brief discussion guide of some questions you might want to consider on your own or with others. The guide is available at no cost from www.ManagaingHorizons.com/press.

In addition, I would be happy to talk with your group, book store, or library in person or virtually. You can contact me at press@ManagingHorizons.com.

Gil Herman

About The Author

Professionally, Gil Herman has been a consultant and executive coach to CEOs and Key Executives in over 200 organizations. His supportive questioning techniques helps his clients define their own challenges and create their own solutions. Philosophically, Gil has continually examined the meaning of life, the universe and everything. Personally, Gil has been married to Meg for more than 50 years and they live in Oak Park, Illinois. Gil is also self-taught on classical guitar.